The King's Quest

The King's Quest

Paul McCusker

PUBLISHING
Colorado Springs, Colorado

Library of Congress Cataloging-in-Publication Data
McCusker, Paul,   1958–
    The king's quest / Paul McCusker.
        p.   cm.—(Adventures in Odyssey; 6)
    Summary: Taking another trip in the Imagination Station, Mark assists the valiant
knight Sir Owwen in his quest for the Ring of Uther and comes to understand God's eternal plan.
    ISBN 1-56179-167-9
    [1. Knights and knighthood—Fiction.   2. Fantasy.   3. Christian life—Fiction.
4. Arthur, King—Fiction.]   I. Title. II. Series: McCusker, Paul, 1958–   Adventures in Odyssey; 6.
PZ7.M47841635Ki   1994
[Fic]–dc20   93-42883
                                                                              CIP
                                                                              AC

Published by Focus on the Family Publishing, Colorado Springs, CO 80920.

Distributed in the U.S.A. and Canada by Word Books, Dallas, Texas.

This is a work of fiction, and any resemblance between the characters in this book and real
persons is coincidental.

Editor: Larry K. Weeden
Interior Illustrations: Jeff Stoddard
Cover Illustration: Jeff Haynie

Printed in the United States of America
   95 96 97 98/10 9 8 7 6 5 4 3

For Elizabeth Sarah Duffield,
who heightened my love and respect for the British
by becoming my wife.

Fans of the audio and video series of **Adventures in Odyssey** *may wonder why some of their favorite characters aren't found in these novels. The answer is simple: the novels take place in a period of time prior to the audio or video series.*

Contents

CHAPTER ONE

A Surprise

Mark was speechless. His mouth hung open, as if someone had just slapped him in the face. His normally pale cheeks turned crimson. His brown eyes were wide with disbelief.

Across the kitchen table, his parents sat side by side. They watched Mark anxiously as their hands clasped tightly on the tabletop. "What did you think would happen when your father and I got back together?" Julie Prescott asked.

Mark chewed his lower lip. "I didn't think . . . I mean, I never figured . . . you know . . ." He carelessly rubbed the side of his head with his palm, making his dark brown hair stick out.

Richard Prescott leaned toward Mark. His brow was deeply furrowed, as if he were contemplating a particularly difficult

1

math problem. Face to face, the resemblance between the two was undeniable; Mark was certainly the younger version of his father. They wore the same expression of thoughtfulness. They shared the same laugh lines around their eyes, noticeable even when they weren't laughing.

"Son," Richard began, "your stay here was only supposed to be temporary."

"But I just got used to being in Odyssey," Mark complained. "And now you want me to leave."

"Your home is in Washington, D.C. It's time to go back," his father said.

Julie nodded and added, "I know it's hard, Mark. But you want us to be together again, right?"

Mark looked down. His fingers were tangled in his lap, little worms that moved nervously back and forth against each other. "It's not fair," he said.

Richard spread his arms as if appealing to Mark. "Can't you just think of it as a . . . a summer vacation? That's all it was. And now it's time to go back home, back to school."

"We'll come visit Odyssey again. I promise," Julie offered.

Mark folded his arms and imagined the packing, the good-byes to all his friends. No more John Avery Whittaker—Whit—with his wild, white hair, bushy eyebrows, and thick mustache that lifted high with his bottomless laugh and bunched up with heartfelt concern. No more Whit's End with its ice cream counter or rooms packed with endless amounts of fun and adventure. No more Patti Eldridge with her freckles and baseball cap pulled down over her sandy hair. No more small-town smiles, friendly handshakes, walks in McCalister Park, or swims in Trickle Lake. No more Odyssey.

"Can't *you* move *here?*" Mark asked his father.

Richard laughed. "And do what? What kind of work would I find in a small town like this?"

"If we thought real hard, I'll bet we could figure something out," Mark said.

Richard shook his head. "No, Mark. Don't even try. We're leaving Odyssey. We're going home to be a family again."

"When?" Mark asked.

"In a couple of weeks," his father answered.

"A couple of weeks!" Mark cried out. "That's too soon!"

"It's the end of the summer," Julie said. "We have to get back to Washington before school starts."

"It'll take that long to make all the arrangements. And that'll give you time to get used to the idea," said Richard.

"I won't get used to it!" Mark pouted as he pushed his chair back and stood up. "I'll *never* get used to it! It's not fair!"

"Mark!"

"No! It's not fair! It's just not fair!" he shouted as the fury bubbled out from inside him like a warm Coke bottle that's been shaken and then opened.

He raced down the hall and out the front door. The screen door slammed like a gunshot behind him, scattering the birds in a nearby tree. His bike lay near the fence. He jerked it up and climbed like a cowboy onto a horse. Up and down, up and down, his legs strained against the resistance of the pedals, then around and around. He pushed hard, gaining speed on the road to downtown Odyssey. The whir of the tires made him pump his legs still harder. He knew where he had to go. He knew what he had to do.

CHAPTER TWO

One Way Out

From the distance across McCalister Park, Whit's End looked like a bunch of misshapen boxes and tubes thrown on top of each other. On closer inspection, the boxes and tubes became walls and turrets and even had a section that looked like an old church. There were reasons for the design, Whit once explained to Mark. "Whit's End is simply a very large house that followed a typical Victorian design," Whit said. "Except for the church, of course. It's from an earlier time."

Mark dropped his bike outside and ran into the building. He stopped just inside the door and looked around. Kids played with displays and various hands-on inventions that Whit strategically placed in all corners. It hummed with all the activity but without the chaos of fun houses and arcades.

Mark glanced at the ice cream counter. Parents and children were crowded onto the stools, at the tables, and in booths, licking ice cream cones or sucking on straws jabbed into milkshakes. A young man Mark didn't recognize happily moved behind the counter, taking orders and answering questions about flavors. Whit often had temporary help. With all the inventing and planning he had to do to keep Whit's End fun and exciting, he needed it. But Whit wasn't there.

Mark quickly walked through the shop, peeking into the many rooms filled with more games, more displays, a complete library, and an enormous train set. Still no sign of Whit. Mark was distressed. He had to talk to him about moving away. He had to see if Whit could come up with an idea that might keep them in Odyssey.

After he exhausted the rooms where Whit was most likely to be found, Mark made his way to the door that led down to Whit's workroom. Few of the kids would have dared enter, but Mark had once worked for Whit and felt he was entitled to go into those special places. He walked down the stairs and stopped at the bottom landing. The room was even more cluttered than when he had last seen it. Apart from the wall-long workbench covered with tools and equipment, the shelves and floor looked like a junkyard of half-finished toys, gizmos, and gadgets that only Whit could identify, including coils and springs, boxes and clocks, electronic wires, and disassembled devices.

In the center of the floor sat a giant contraption that looked like a cross between a telephone booth and a helicopter cockpit. For someone who didn't know better, the machine's dark glass and thick, silver plating made it look as invincible as a bank safe and as threatening as an armored tank. But Mark knew better.

It was The Imagination Station.

Whit had created it so kids could travel through time to learn about the Bible and history. Mark wasn't sure how it worked or whether it could really move people through time. But he once had an experience of his own in it, and the adventure seemed real enough.

Mark often wondered when Whit would take The Imagination Station out of the workroom and put it where the kids could use it, but Whit always answered the same way: "I still have some tinkering to do with it." And tinkering was the very thing Whit was doing when Mark walked around to the back side of the machine.

"Hello, Mark!" Whit said cheerfully as he tugged at a stubborn bolt with a wrench. "How are you?"

"Not very good," Mark said. "What are you doing?"

"Just trying to—" he grunted and tugged again—"finish a little program that I—" tug and jerk—"put into The Imagination Station."

"A *new* program?" Mark asked.

The bolt gave up the fight, and Whit spun it loose from the plate. "I've been trying several different ideas," Whit said. He sat back and scratched at his white mane. "What do you mean you're not very good?"

Mark shrugged and answered, "My mom and dad told me we have to move away from Odyssey."

"Oh," Whit said softly.

"You knew, didn't you?" Mark asked, a hint of accusation in his voice. "You knew that if my mom and dad got back together, this would happen."

Whit brushed at his nose with the side of his hand and looked up at Mark. "Yes, I did."

"Why didn't you tell me?"

"Because your parents needed to tell you," Whit said.

"But what am I going to do?" Mark asked, realizing now that the thing he didn't do at home he might do here. He was going to cry.

"Mark," Whit said as he climbed to his feet. "Deep in your heart, you must've known."

Mark shook his head as his eyes welled up. "I didn't. Honest, I didn't."

Whit pulled Mark close. There, in the warmth and comfort of that embrace, Mark released the tears. They came gently at first, then spilled out in hard sobs.

"This is how it is, Mark," Whit said quietly. His low voice resonated through his chest to where Mark's ear was pressed. "We rarely get the good things without the bad. You were miserable when you first came to Odyssey, remember?"

Mark nodded his head yes.

"Your parents had split up, and all you could think about was getting them back together and living in Washington again. Well, that's what happened. Your prayers were answered."

"But it's not fair," Mark sniffled. "I've been here all summer. I like it here."

"And I'm sure you'll come back again," Whit said.

"I don't want to leave," Mark said, crying again. "If I prayed to go, then I can pray to stay, too."

Whit held him for a moment longer, then stepped back at arm's length, his hands on Mark's shoulders. He looked him full in the face and said, "You know prayer doesn't work like that, Mark. God isn't some genie who grants you wishes. Whatever happens to you happens because it fits into His plan for you. It's a plan filled with His love and goodness."

"It's still not fair," Mark declared.

"Maybe it isn't fair. And maybe it doesn't seem right," Whit said. "But I believe with all my heart that, for those who love God, everything happens for the good. Even when we make mistakes, God will turn them around for our benefit."

Within his mind and heart, Mark struggled to believe it. Whit was kind and wise and would never lead Mark astray. He wouldn't say things just to make Mark feel better. Whit was speaking the truth. But Mark's emotions — tangled like weeds around a rosebush — choked off his better sense. *If* God really had some sort of plan, leaving Odyssey couldn't possibly be part of it. God was making some kind of mistake.

"I have an idea," Whit said, and he knelt next to The Imagination Station.

Mark watched him curiously.

"I think this program may help you understand better than anything I could say." Whit reached into the empty square where the panel was removed and set to work.

"What do you mean?" Mark asked.

"You're taking a trip in The Imagination Station," Whit answered.

CHAPTER THREE

Another Time

The door to The Imagination Station closed with a deep, resonant boom. Mark settled into the cushioned chair and watched the flashing lights on the control panel. Once again, he was struck by how much they'd changed since he was last inside. Whit had been doing a lot of work.

"Are you comfortable?" Whit asked, his voice thin and hollow as it came through the tiny intercom speaker.

"Yeah, I guess," Mark replied.

"Good," Whit said. "If you need anything, just let me know."

"Okay."

The intercom speaker crackled, then Whit said, "You can go ahead and push the red button when you're ready."

Mark looked at the control panel. The red button sat prominently in the center. It flashed at him expectantly. "You mean *this* button?" Mark asked and pushed it.

The power surge took Mark by surprise, making him feel as if the machine were being thrust forward while pushing him back into his seat. *Am I really moving?* he wondered. The Imagination Station whined, rattled, and bounced. Mark wasn't alarmed, but it made his stomach do flips as if he were on a roller-coaster ride.

Through the speaker, Mark heard Whit's voice — surely a recording of some sort — counting backward from ten. As he reached "three . . . two . . . one," he paused and then said, "Once upon a time . . ."

The Imagination Station slowed down, then settled into a soft hum. The door opened by itself.

Sunlight momentarily blinded Mark as he climbed out of the cockpit. He blinked once or twice while his other senses told him he wasn't in the workroom at Whit's End anymore. Gone was the hard cement of Whit's workroom against the bottom of his feet. He had stepped onto a dirt floor, wet and slippery. The smells of moldy straw, horse manure, and rotten wood also accosted him.

And the sounds! He heard a peculiar, metallic rattling, followed by the sharp clanging of steel on steel. Identifying the clanging was easy. It was as if someone were banging a sledgehammer against an anvil. *Ching!* The sound was unmistakable. Mark had heard it thousands of times in old movies. It was a sword fight!

Where in the world am I?

Mark squinted through the bright light and saw he was in an abandoned shack. A wood table and chairs had been carelessly tossed against a wall. No doubt, animals had taken shelter in here at some time. The door, made of wooden boards that termites and rot had long since given up on, hung indifferently from a single hinge at the top of the doorpost. There were no windows.

An abandoned shack, he mused. *But where?*

The constant *ching! ching! ching!* of the sword fight came from outside, and Mark crept to the door. Carefully, he opened it wide enough to get a peek. What he saw took his breath away. Against a backdrop of a green field, grove of trees, and brilliant, blue sky, two men dressed in knight's armor — one suit black, one silver — danced around each other, swords poised for attack.

This isn't Odyssey anymore, Mark knew. Though he had once been to a traveling Renaissance festival that put on pageants, jousts, and battles between knights in shining armor, he couldn't imagine what any of this scene had to do with moving back to Washington, D.C. Maybe Whit made a mistake. The Imagination Station wasn't foolproof. And unlike the sparkling knights of playacting, these fellows weren't shining at all. Their armor was dented and dirty.

The knight in black armor threw himself forward with a wide swipe of the blade. The other knight sidestepped and countered with a hard blow to his opponent's back. The movement caused their armor to rattle loudly, and Mark recognized it as the sound he had heard from inside. As the black knight swung around to face his opponent again, the silver knight retaliated with a fierce stab that deflected off the chest plate and struck the black knight's shoulder, piercing the chain mail. The black knight cried out and stumbled backward.

Mark expected the silver knight to follow this thrust with another, but he didn't. Instead, he slumped where he was, as if trying to catch his breath. The black knight swung himself around, allowing the momentum to bring the flat of his sword crashing against the silver knight's side.

The two knights are tired, Mark thought. Not only did they gasp and groan as they struck and parried, but they also held their swords as if each weighed a ton. The armor surely didn't help. It — and the chain mail underneath — covered them from head to foot and seemed to hamper their every move. They looked like a couple of poorly designed puppets in the hands of a bad puppeteer.

Mark then realized that the entire scene seemed to glisten in the light. But it wasn't the glistening of water or dew; the shine came from the blood of the two men. The armor, the chain mail, and even the grass seemed sprayed with red.

"This is real!" Mark gasped.

The silver knight propelled himself forward again — a bad move. His weak legs suddenly slipped out from under him, probably from the wet grass, and threw him onto his back. The black knight lifted his sword high.

"No!" Mark gasped, jerking his hands to his face. His arm knocked against the door, and it creaked loudly as it moved another inch. It was more than the poor hinge could take. Barely clinging to the wood of the frame, it now wrenched free and sent the door falling with a splintering crash.

The black knight, startled from his sure victory, turned in Mark's direction. That gave the silver knight the moment he desperately needed. He brought his sword up with all his might and pushed it between two separate sections of the black knight's armor.

The black knight clutched the blade with his metal gloves and cried out. The silver knight pulled the blade out, rolling aside as a precaution in case the black knight had the strength to fight back.

Mark pressed his hands against his mouth to restrain the scream perched at the back of his throat.

"You will not succeed," the black knight gasped, frozen in place. Then he swayed like a branch in a gentle breeze, fell to his knees, and collapsed face forward onto the ground.

The silver knight looked down at his enemy and jabbed the lifeless body with his toe. Satisfied that the black knight posed no further threat, he turned toward Mark. "Boy! Come out!" he called.

Mark fearfully stepped back into the shack.

"Did you not hear me? I said to come out!" the silver knight shouted. His voice was thick and husky, and he spoke with a British accent. The knight came toward Mark.

Mark retreated farther into the shack, quickly glancing around to see if he had a way of escape. A wooden ladder led upward to a loft. Mark raced for it.

The knight's armor rattled with each step, getting closer and closer while Mark scrambled to the top of the ladder. He had barely made it into the loft — a rotten-smelling, straw-covered platform — when the knight entered the shack. "Boy!" he cried out.

Mark checked all sides and saw there weren't any windows at this level, either. He had nowhere to go. He was trapped.

"Boy!" the knight shouted.

Mark scampered to the farthest point from the ladder and crouched in a dark corner, hoping the shadows would hide him.

Suddenly the knight cried out. Mark heard an enormous clatter and crash of armor, then silence. The knight moaned.

Mark thought it might be some sort of trick and waited a moment. "Uhhh," the knight continued to moan from somewhere below.

Unable to resist his curiosity, Mark cautiously crept to the edge of the loft and peered over.

The knight had apparently stumbled over the fallen door and now lay still beside it. Whether he was hurt or simply exhausted, Mark couldn't tell. All that mattered, for the moment, was that Mark was safe.

Until the loft collapsed.

CHAPTER FOUR

King's Quest

When Mark came to his senses again, he found himself on a small bed in a room of rough stone walls. A narrow window above his head allowed a shaft of sunlight to illuminate a colorful coat of arms hanging directly opposite. The coat of arms had four crudely painted squares. The first contained a red dragon, the second a roaring lion, the third a white dove, and the fourth a red rose.

He lifted his hand to his aching head, only to feel the coarse cloth of a bandage wrapped snugly there. It took him a moment to remember what had happened, and, once he did, he sat up and tossed the blanket aside. *I have to get out of here*, he thought, certain the silver knight would come clanking along at any minute to hurt him.

The door opened, and a woman dressed like a nun came in

17

carrying a tray. She stopped when she saw Mark was sitting up, muttered something he couldn't hear, then quickly ran out again.

Mark seized the chance to escape and sprinted to the door, his feet and head pounding along the way. He made it as far as the doorway before he realized he was wearing only his underwear!

He gasped and doubled back to the bed to grab a blanket for covering. He wrapped it around himself and returned to the door — just in time to be intercepted by a tall, distinguished-looking man with long, gray hair and a tangled beard.

"Well, God be praised!" said the man warmly as he placed a firm hand on Mark's shoulder and guided him back to the bed. "We feared for your good health, lad, so severe was the fall you took."

Mark sat down on the bed again. The man grabbed a small, wooden chair and pulled it close. Mark noticed he was dressed in a long, brown robe, fringed with a gold and blue design. On his shoulders hung a red cape, which he wrapped around himself as he sat down. A bony foot clad in a sandal emerged from under the robe.

"Where am I?" Mark asked.

"You are in my castle," the man answered with a smile, speaking with the same sort of accent as the knight had earlier.

"But who are you?"

"I am Sir Miles of Brandon, master of this castle and the

surrounding lands to the Great River." The man did not move but sat perfectly still and looked intently at Mark.

"Are you the knight who — who —" Mark didn't want to say the word *killed*, but he couldn't think of a good replacement. Sir Miles shook his head. "Alas, I would that I had the strength and courage of that great knight. In my younger days, yes, but no longer. Sir Owwen is the one of whom you speak. A man of knightly courage and honor. He brought you here."

"He did?" Mark asked, surprised.

"Yes." Sir Miles leaned back and folded his arms across his chest. "Tell me your name, lad, and from whence you come."

"I'm Mark Prescott," he answered. "From Odyssey."

"Odyssey?"

Mark nodded. "Do you know where it is?"

"I fear not," Sir Miles said. "But I suspect it is a great distance by your strange accent."

"*My* strange accent!" Mark said.

Sir Miles scratched his chin, chuckled, and added, "And your clothes."

"Oh, yeah. Can I have them back now?"

"If they are dry, you may," Sir Miles said and clapped his hands. "Your fall landed you in some very potent-smelling dung. I have asked my servants to wash them."

"Thanks," Mark said.

A different woman from the one who came in before entered. Sir Miles gestured to Mark, and the woman bowed obediently and left. Afterward, Sir Miles smiled and said,

"Your raiment has caused quite a disturbance in my household. All the servants want to see your clothes. Your tunic —"

"Tunic?"

Sir Miles plucked at his chest and repeated, "Tunic."

"My *shirt!*" Mark said, proud of himself for understanding.

"Never have I seen round clasps of such strange making. With holes!" Sir Miles said.

Mark figured he was talking about the plastic buttons and said so. Sir Miles repeated the word *button* the way a child might say *Mama*— again and again.

Sir Miles's servant girl returned with Mark's clothes, now dried by the fire in the kitchen, and Mark found himself playing "show and tell" with his jeans (which Sir Miles called "leggings") and socks ("very short tights").

After the servant girl left, Mark got dressed while Sir Miles watched. "This is a wonder to me!" he finally shouted. "Must you always work so hard to dress? Do you not have simpler tunics and robes in your land?"

"We have robes," Mark replied defensively. "But we wear them around the house, not outside. May I have my shoes now?"

"Ah!" Sir Miles said and reached under the bed. He pulled out Mark's tennis shoes and held them up reverently in both hands as if he cradled two precious jewels. "Your footwear is white and made of . . . of . . . what is this?" He rubbed his finger against the sole.

"Rubber," Mark answered.

"Rubber," Sir Miles repeated softly. "From whence does this rubber come?"

Mark shrugged and took the shoes. "The factory, I guess. You'll have to ask my mom."

Sir Miles opened his mouth to say something else, but he was interrupted by the arrival of another man. He was as tall as Sir Miles but of a younger, stronger build. His hair and beard were dark and curly and set off his penetrating, pale blue eyes. He wore a large, white vest over black chain mail. On the front of the vest was sewn a pattern of upside-down V shapes in alternating colors of red and yellow.

"Sir Owwen!" Sir Miles shouted happily, leaping to his feet. "How do you fare? Are your wounds dressed satisfactorily?"

Sir Owwen bowed slightly in a gesture of respect. "Sit down, good friend," he said. "My wounds are healing, and I am refreshed thanks to your great courtesy. Thanks be to God that I was victorious over the evil knight who sought my life."

"Praise to God," Sir Miles affirmed.

Sir Owwen turned to Mark and said, "But I would be remiss to mention that victory without saying that it was due primarily to the miraculous and timely arrival of this boy."

Mark was tempted to look behind him, sure that Sir Owwen was talking about someone else.

"You, lad, saved my life and, in doing so, have served our great king in ways you cannot know," Sir Owwen said. "I kneel before you now in gratitude."

Mark blushed and looked helplessly at Sir Miles, who smiled back at him.

Sir Owwen lowered his head and said, "I am your servant if ever you have need of help . . . er, by what name are you called?"

"Mark Prescott," Mark said.

"Of Odyssey," Sir Miles added.

"Mark Prescott of Odyssey," Sir Owwen said, then stood up. "I depart now to continue my quest for the king." He turned on his heel to leave but suddenly stopped. "Odyssey?" he said. "Is that the place from which you come?"

Mark nodded.

Sir Owwen's expression changed to one of amazement.

"Have you heard of it, Sir Owwen?" asked Sir Miles.

"Yes, I have," Sir Owwen replied. He leaned and whispered something in Sir Miles's ear. Sir Miles listened attentively, scratched his chin, then instantly sped from the room. Sir Owwen sat down in the chair next to Mark. In a hushed voice, he explained that the king had told him he would meet someone from Odyssey — a most peculiar thing to say since, to Sir Owwen's knowledge, no such place existed.

"That's weird," Mark said. "How could he know you'd meet someone from Odyssey? I didn't even know I was coming until right before I arrived."

Sir Owwen leaned forward and rested his stubbly chin on the back of his large, callused hands. "In what manner did you arrive? For I searched that shack myself prior to the sudden attack by the black knight, and surely it was empty. You could only have entered through the door, on which I had my eyes set. I didn't see you."

"The Imagination Station," Mark answered.

Sir Owwen cocked his head as if trying to interpret the words, then seemed to give up. "By whatever means you were sent, I can only believe you are a living sign from God in this, my quest for the king. Are you strong enough to travel?"

The possibility of adventure and excitement overtook his better sense, and he jumped up. "Yeah!" Mark said.

"Then let us be on our way!" Sir Owwen shouted heartily. He stood up quickly, knocking the chair over as he did.

As they strode down the long, stone hallway, Mark asked Sir Owwen what exactly their quest was.

Sir Owwen quickly glanced around to be sure they weren't being spied upon, then tilted his enormous frame toward Mark. "We must rescue the Ring of Uther from Slothgrowl!" he whispered.

"Who's Slothgrowl?" Mark asked.

Sir Owwen looked at Mark with disbelief. "Is it possible you have not heard of Slothgrowl?" he asked.

"Honest, I haven't," Mark said. "Who is he?"

"Only the most evil and ferocious dragon in the land!"

CHAPTER FIVE

Squire Mark

Mark and Sir Owwen walked along seemingly endless stone corridors and down innumerable steps before emerging from the dark and damp castle into daylight. Even then, they were still well inside the fortress walls. Men and women moved to and fro, engrossed in their business. Occasionally someone would stop to notice Sir Owwen or to stare at Mark's clothes. He didn't realize how much he stood out until he noticed that the other men wore brown tunics with a belt, matching leggings, and ragged leather boots. The women wore long dresses and scarves on their heads.

Mark followed Sir Owwen across the courtyard. He later learned that it was called the inner ward and contained the homes of Sir Miles, his family, and servants. It was an odd collection of stone walls and half-timber apartments.

They continued through the inner gatehouse to the outer ward, where guards watched their progress. Mark stumbled once or twice over small children and fleeing chickens who got under his feet when he was staring upward at the gigantic, rounded towers sitting on each corner of the wards.

"I've never been in a castle before," Mark said breathlessly. Mark hoped Sir Owwen would take it as a hint to slow down and let him look around.

Sir Owwen simply grunted and strode on.

At the outer gatehouse, by far the largest in the castle, complete with a drawbridge and moat, they were met by Sir Miles and the two servants Mark had seen earlier. It was clear now why Sir Miles hastily left the room. He had assembled provisions for them — satchels of food and Sir Owwen's freshly cleaned armor (still dented) — all strapped to a packhorse named Kevin.

"Why Kevin?" Mark asked.

"It is the same name as the fiend I drove out of this castle two score years ago," Sir Miles explained.

Mark wanted to hear the story behind that battle, but Sir Owwen interrupted to bid Sir Miles a warm farewell. He took Kevin by the reins and walked across the drawbridge. The sound of Kevin's hooves seemed to bounce in all directions off the castle walls.

"Thanks for everything," Mark said to Sir Miles. Then he ran along the edge of the drawbridge to get a look below. He thought he might see alligators in the moat. Instead, he saw (and smelled) only stagnant water, thick with mud and green slime.

Once they were clear of the drawbridge, Mark and Sir Owwen followed the dirt road through a small village. From homes and shops made of half-timber, wattle (woven sticks), and daub (mud and clay), the villagers came out to proclaim Sir Owwen a "brave knight" and to wish him "godspeed." At Mark, they simply stared.

"They believe you to be my squire," Sir Owwen said as they passed the smiling and waving villagers.

"Squire? What's that?" Mark asked.

"My attendant," Sir Owwen answered.

"*Squire* Mark Prescott," Mark whispered to himself again and again, as if trying it on for size. "Squire Mark. Cool!"

Beyond the village, the road stretched out across a field and disappeared into a thick forest. Mark scanned the panorama and took a deep breath. The colors were so vivid to him; he had never seen so many greens, yellows, and browns. Or a sky so blue or a sun so bright.

"Where are we?" Mark wondered aloud.

"We are departing from the castle and village of Brandon," answered Sir Owwen.

"I mean the country," Mark said.

"Truly, do you not know?" Sir Owwen asked, bewildered.

"I didn't know where Whit was sending me," Mark replied. "He just said to get in, so I did."

"You are in the great country of Albion, blessed by God and favored in His blessings." Sir Owwen beamed.

"Is it real or made up?"

Sir Owwen said indignantly, "Real or made up? Do you question the truth of what I speak?"

"No! But . . . how could this place be real if you have dragons?" asked Mark.

"Stand face to face with Slothgrowl and my young liege will know its reality," Sir Owwen said with a chuckle. He went on to add that Slothgrowl was a hideous monster with snakelike skin, except for a patch of scales found just beneath his neck that were said to be made of a substance harder than iron in order to protect his heart. He had talons at the end of each of his four legs. As for his face, it was long and oily with tiny, red eyes, large, cannonlike nostrils, and razor-sharp teeth that were said to bite through the thickest armor.

Mark shuddered, and even Kevin snorted and shook his head, as if scared by what he heard. "So why is the Ring of Uther so important that you'd risk your life trying to get it?"

Sir Owwen patted Kevin on the neck. "That is a great secret which only the king himself can answer. It is enough for me to obey his highness and retrieve the ring, if God so wills it."

"But *why?*" Mark persisted. It was hard for him to understand obedience without explanation.

"Why?" Sir Owwen echoed. "Would I dare offend the king by questioning his commands?"

"You mean you'd do *anything* he wanted you to do?"

"I have sworn allegiance to my king—even to the death," Sir Owwen replied.

"But what if this whole ring business is a mistake?" Mark asked.

Sir Owwen stopped and looked carefully at Mark. "Perhaps *I* was mistaken in bringing you along. The king is a wise and just monarch whom I follow wholeheartedly. Unfortunately, not all in the kingdom agree, and some would overthrow him if they could. The evil knight I defeated earlier is but one of them. He suddenly attacked me as I rode on this quest of the king's."

"How did he know who you were?"

"By my colors and my horse," Sir Owwen said. "Alas, when he attacked, he murdered that good and faithful animal. I suspect the evil knight knew of my purpose and was sent to thwart my undertaking."

Mark shrugged. "Must be a pretty important ring."

"We must be on guard at all times, young Mark," Sir Owwen stated earnestly. "For this quest is not only of flesh and blood, but even more of the spirit! Forces of the darkest kind may be rallying against us. Even sorcery."

"You mean *magic?*"

Sir Owwen nodded somberly and made the sign of the cross with his hand. "We fight not only for our bodies, but also for our souls."

CHAPTER SIX

The Woman
in the Woods

B y this time, Mark, Sir Owwen, and a wary-looking Kevin
had entered the forest. The thick tangle of branches
formed a canopy over their heads that nearly blocked out
all sunlight. It took Mark a moment to adjust his eyes. A fox
ran in front of them, stopped long enough to bark, then fled
into the thicket.

"How did Slothgrowl get hold of the ring in the first place?"
Mark asked softly, as if his voice could awaken unwanted com-
panions who might be asleep in the many shadows of the wood.

Sir Owwen explained that it was stolen from the king's
castle by a shrewd enchantress, who took on the appearance of
one of the king's servants to gain access to the treasured ring.
Neither the ring nor the enchantress had been seen since. Most
people suspected she was in league with Slothgrowl.

31

"Where is Slothgrowl now?" asked Mark, unable to get rid of the image of the dragon in his mind.

"That I do not know," answered Sir Owwen. "No one knows. Slothgrowl rides on dragon mist and can only be seen by those with the eyes to see."

"Then how are *we* going to find him?" Mark inquired.

"By faith," Sir Owwen replied.

"That's it?"

"The king has given me specific things for which to look," Sir Owwen said. "The first sign was to prepare for the sudden appearance of a mysterious stranger who would speak of Odyssey."

Mark shivered unexpectedly. He still couldn't imagine how he was the first sign in an adventure that he had only just joined. "What was the second sign?" Mark asked.

Sir Owwen said, "It will be the discovery and recovery of the Sword of Scales. It is the only sword that can kill Slothgrowl."

"Great!" Mark said cheerfully. "Where is the Sword of Scales?"

"No one knows," Sir Owwen said sadly. "It has been missing for years, longer than I have had breath in my body. Some suspect that an evil lord is keeping it hidden so Slothgrowl can continue to prowl the land without fear."

Mark cocked an eyebrow at Sir Owwen. "So we're looking for a dragon that no one can find in order to kill him with a sword no one can find?"

Sir Owwen tugged at one of the curls near his ear. "Aye," he said.

They walked on in silence for most of the day, covering quite a long distance, until they heard a sound echo through the woods. At first Mark thought it was the wind in the trees, but then he was chilled to realize it was a human noise. Somewhere a woman wailed, low and mournful, broken only by wrenching sobs. Kevin lurched backward so that Sir Owwen had to yank at the rein to steady him.

"What is it?" Mark whispered. His question was a hope for assurance that they weren't about to encounter one of the dark forces Sir Owwen had mentioned.

"Clearly a woman," Sir Owwen replied as he pressed onward.

They rounded a bend in the road and saw her. She sat upon a log, dressed in rags, weeping profusely with her face in her hands. Her blonde hair was matted and streaked with dirt. She didn't look up as they approached.

"Woman!" Sir Owwen called out. "Pray, why do you weep so that the very branches stoop to mourn?"

She lifted her head slightly and cried, "Alas, sir knight, I am a poor widow of a kind and generous woodsman. He was killed on this very spot one year ago by blackguards in the service of Sir Cardoc, who desired only our land. They cast my only son and myself out into the woods, where we have wandered, scrounging food from the forest, as our only means by which to live. Until this very day —" She choked on her words and began to weep again.

Sir Owwen directed a wary look to Mark, then knelt next to the woman. "Speak, damsel. What events took place this day that should cause you to weep so horribly?"

She mustered her courage and looked fully into their faces. *Under different circumstances,* Mark thought, *she would be beautiful.* He figured she couldn't have been much older than his own mother, which probably meant her son was about his age.

"They took him!" she sobbed. "They took my son!"

Sir Owwen placed his hand on his heart, lowered his head, sighed deeply, and said, "God, have mercy."

"The wicked Sir Cardoc has taken him as a slave to his castle just beyond these woods," she said. "Woe is me, that I should have lived to see such ends!"

"Why don't you call the police?" Mark asked.

Both the woman and Sir Owwen looked at him quizzically.

"Okay, so maybe you don't have police now," he amended. "But maybe we can rescue him!" Mark turned to Sir Owwen and asked, "Can't we?"

The woman gazed at them hopefully.

Sir Owwen reddened and stammered, "My squire is young and ignorant of his words, though his heart be in the proper place."

"What does that mean?" Mark asked.

"That we should counsel one with another before making

hasty vows," Sir Owwen said. Then he guided Mark by the arm to the opposite side of the path.

"You don't want to help her?" Mark asked in a hoarse whisper.

"With my whole heart, I desire nothing more," Sir Owwen said. "But my quest is for the king. He bade me to be wary of strangers seeking help, for they might lure me away from my higher purpose."

Mark frowned. "But look at her!" he said. "She's not luring anybody. She just needs help. You're a hotshot knight! You know how to rescue people from castles, don't you?"

Sir Owwen shook his head as he replied, "In the name of justice, I would die trying. But I must remember the king!"

"Are you telling me the king wouldn't want you to help her?" Mark asked pointedly.

Sir Owwen glanced at the woman thoughtfully, then back at Mark. His eyes reflected the inner struggle he waged.

"If you won't help her, *I* will!" Mark announced. He had no idea where all this sudden bravery came from. Maybe it was caused by standing in these thick woods, so full of wonder and mystery. Or maybe it came from this time of valiant knights, dangerous dragons, and damsels in distress. Whatever it was, Mark felt capable of accomplishing anything.

Sir Owwen knelt, bowed his head, and prayed softly. After a moment, he whispered "Amen" and stood up. "Be it folly or valor," he announced, "we will do our utmost to rescue this fair woman's son."

CHAPTER SEVEN

The Great Castle of Cardoc

It was evening before Sir Owwen and Mark came up with a plan. Borrowing the clothes of the woman's dead husband, Sir Owwen made himself out to be a traveling merchant. Then they covered Mark's "peculiar-looking garments" with an outfit owned by the missing boy and left Kevin and their provisions at the woman's makeshift lean-to in the woods.

"Are you sure this'll work?" Mark asked as he adjusted his tunic.

"By God's grace," Sir Owwen replied. Even in his costume of a rusty brown tunic and patched cloak, he looked imposing.

Yet Mark's heart pounded and his mouth went dry as they emerged from the forest and approached the gate to the great castle of Cardoc. Torches burned on both sides of the open gate, which yawned at them from across the drawbridge and the black moat underneath. Sir Owwen grabbed Mark's arm and jerked him along every step to the gate itself, where they were met by a guard.

"What business have you here?" the guard asked coarsely.

Sir Owwen pushed Mark forward. "What business does any man have being robbed by beggar boys like this! I want justice done by the lord of these lands!" he demanded.

"Justice!" The guard laughed and gestured them through. "Yes, we shall see to justice. Sir Cardoc is in the great hall. Follow me!"

Again Sir Owwen grabbed Mark by the arm, and he led him through the courtyard. It was a dazzling sight to Mark. Unlike the courtyard at Sir Miles's castle, with its shacks and houses, this courtyard was full of booths, carts, and stalls, as if it were the meeting place of a giant market. People milled about, but they weren't idle. They gathered in pockets around men and women who performed by torchlight. Some juggled knives, others played instruments that looked like small guitars and long flutes, while acrobats flung themselves head over heels through the crowd or balanced lances on the tips of their noses. It was like a circus.

Sir Owwen pulled Mark close. "Sir Cardoc is celebrating a market meeting," he whispered. "A better means for our escape."

They followed the guard down a short corridor and through a large arch leading into the expanse of the great hall. And great it was! It stretched almost 100 feet ahead and must have been 50 feet wide. The dark, gray stones reached high up to rafters that disappeared into blackness. Each wall had two or three fireplaces, all burning brightly with huge fires. Tapestries and heraldries decorated other portions of the walls. Tables surrounded by men and women spread lengthwise toward the end of the room, where the largest table of all spanned the hall from side to side. Obviously, the large table — the "high table," it was called — was the place of honor.

As the guard led them past the many tables, Mark saw that the men and women were eating roasted meat on silver plates, but without forks or spoons. They used their fingers and ripped at the brown mutton with their teeth. Drinks were served in pewter cups. Horns of plenty decorated the centers of the tables, each filled with berries.

The floor itself was covered with rushes, and Mark nearly got nipped by the dogs and cats who fought over the odd scraps of food the dinner guests threw to them.

At the high table, the men and women dressed in more-colorful clothes and were obviously of greater rank than their guests. The guard took Mark and Sir Owwen front and center, where they looked up at a thin, sharp-featured man with jet-black hair and piercing eyes. But what caught Mark's attention was the long scar that extended from the man's right temple across his cheek to his chin. This was Sir Cardoc.

"My lord," the guard said, "this merchant craves to speak with you."

Sir Cardoc glanced up from the bone he was gnawing. "What does he want?" he asked.

Sir Owwen cleared his throat and said, "Justice, my lord. This beggar boy tried to forcibly rob me as I crossed your land. I beg you for justice."

Sir Cardoc rested his greasy chin on his greasy hands and eyed them both.

Something's wrong, Mark thought. The plan was for Sir Cardoc to throw Mark in the dungeon—most likely the same place containing the woman's son, since castles had only one dungeon beneath the basement. Sir Owwen would then make as if to leave, but instead he would come later in the night, when it was safe, knock out the guard, and rescue both Mark and the boy. But Mark suddenly sensed, *It isn't going to work.*

"I'll give you justice." Sir Cardoc chuckled low and mean. "Guard?"

The guard stepped forward and said, "Yes, my lord?"

Sir Cardoc gestured to Mark with the bone and said, "Kill the boy."

CHAPTER EIGHT

Tricked

The dinner guests went suddenly quiet.

"What!" Mark shouted.

"My lord?" the guard asked, unsure of what he had heard.

"I said to kill the boy!" Sir Cardoc raged. "We have too many beggars around here anyway. It's bad for commerce."

The guard drew his sword, and Sir Owwen placed his hand on it gently. "Sir Cardoc," Sir Owwen said, "I came only for justice, not an execution."

"You said you wanted justice," Sir Cardoc said. "What did you expect, a beating? A time in my dungeon? It's filled to the brim."

"But my lord, I beseech you. As a humble merchant, I would be stricken to bear the responsibility of this boy's death."

Sir Cardoc laughed. "As a humble merchant, did you say? Is that what you said?" Sir Cardoc roared with laughter, and the guests, relieved, joined with him. Then abruptly, he pushed himself back from the table and stood up. His face turned red with rage, and his scar shone like a stream of blood. He pointed his finger at Sir Owwen and shouted, "You are no merchant! You are Sir Owwen, knight and scoundrel! And now you are my prisoner!"

Sir Owwen cried out to Mark, "An ambush! Quickly!" Even as he shouted, he grabbed the guard by the wrist, twisted it so that the sword dropped free, and scooped up the weapon. One deft stroke took care of the guard, and Sir Owwen spun around to face the rest of Sir Cardoc's men. They rushed from all sides, getting entangled with the confused and frightened dinner guests, who decided it was time to skip dessert and go home.

"Sir Owwen!" Mark screamed, panicked and unsure of what to do.

"Run, Mark! Run!"

Mark did. Past people, between legs, over chairs and under tables, he scrambled for a door. Any door. He found one and pushed through, turning back quickly in time to see a dozen men hurl themselves upon Sir Owwen.

"There he is!" another guard shouted, pointing at Mark.

****

The door opened into the kitchen—a large, cluttered room

containing an enormous fireplace where black pots of varying sizes hung above the flames. Pieces of animals and vegetables littered the tables and floor, making everything slippery for Mark as he ran through. The men and women who served Sir Cardoc's guests were too busy to notice the commotion in the great hall. Or maybe they didn't care.

A guard followed Mark into the kitchen. Mark caught sight of him pushing his way between the tables and past the servants just as Mark darted through another door on the opposite side of the room. It led to a small enclosure crowded with clay pots and jars. Mark quickly looked around for a door or window through which to escape, but he didn't see one.

I'm stuck in a closet! Mark thought as he scrambled around the room, his heart racing like a trapped animal's. He returned to the door and peeked out. The guard hadn't seen him leave the kitchen — he pushed over tables and shouted at the servants for not being more observant.

An old woman said something to the guard and pointed to the closet door. Mark closed it and stepped back, glancing around the room for some kind of protection. His eye caught a small, stone edifice in the far corner. It had a wooden covering and a rope tied onto a metal ring.

A well! Mark realized. He lifted the cover and, grabbing the rope, began to lower himself in. He had just disappeared beneath the top when he heard the door crash in and the guard shout, "Come out, you ratbag!"

Mark continued to lower himself along the rope, wondering

how long it would be before he'd touch water. The walls were moist and slimy.

From the noises above, Mark guessed that the guard was knocking over the jars in search of him. He clung to the rope and waited. If the guard gave up and left, Mark could pull himself out.

After a few minutes, the closet above was silent. Mark's arms grew tired, and the moldy smell of the well turned his stomach. He figured he had waited long enough and looked up. All he could see was the ceiling of the room. The muscles in his arms groaned as he pulled on the rope, moving inches upward.

Suddenly the rope jerked. Mark looked up and saw the guard leering down at him. The guard had hold of the rope and was pulling him up!

"Got you, you scamp!" the guard said with a laugh.

Mark frantically lowered himself as the rope was yanked up. The guard was strong, and Mark realized he wasn't making any progress downward. Then his foot bumped against the bucket tied to the end of the rope. Time was running out. Unless Mark let go, the guard would soon have him at the top.

The wet bucket, half filled with water, banged against Mark's knees. He looked down at the black emptiness below.

The guard laughed. "You'll be a nice prize for my master," he said.

Mark looked up again at the leering smile and decided the black emptiness wasn't so bad after all. He let go of the rope.

The guard fell backward from the sudden lack of weight to pull.

Mark hit the water and sank deeper than he expected. He reached out to the well walls, but his arms flailed freely. The walls were gone. He had dropped beyond the bottom of the well and into a reservoir of some sort. He couldn't feel the top, nor did his feet touch bottom.

He opened his eyes and twisted around, hoping that some light might penetrate the darkness. It didn't. He looked up and couldn't see the bottom of the well. He nearly gasped as he realized he didn't know which way to go. His lungs ached.

Pushing himself up with his legs, he kept his hands above his head. They bumped against a cold, stone surface. He carefully felt his way along, praying for a gap of air or another passage. Wet rock met his every touch. His lungs felt like balloons on the brink of explosion.

Mark knew he had to push in one direction or the other if he hoped to survive. Froglike, he pumped his legs and stretched out his arms for whatever waited ahead in the dark water. His lungs screamed for air.

He pushed harder, panicking, even though he knew it was the worst thing to do. His ears began to ring, and he felt black bubbles of unconsciousness bursting around his head.

I'm going to drown in the bottom of this castle, he thought. *They'll never find my body. My parents will never know what happened to me.*

His legs continued to pump automatically. His arms began

to drop. *It's not so bad*, he mused. *It's kind of like falling asleep. If only I could breathe out and breathe in again.*

He exhaled slowly, the bubbles tickling his nose and drifting upward as they left him. He began to sink farther as the air left his body. *Just like falling asleep . . .*

Suddenly, strong hands invaded the water and grabbed Mark's tunic.

CHAPTER NINE

The Old Man

Mark's retching and coughing brought him to full consciousness again. He was flat on his back, pressed against cold stone, his head turned to the side for the water to spill out of his lungs and mouth. When he could open his eyes, he realized he was on a ledge. His arm was carelessly stretched out, dangling above the water. He wiggled his fingers, allowing them to touch the surface. They made sounds like pebbles dropped one by one into a pond.

"Well?" a thin, scratchy voice asked.

Mark snapped his head around and was blinded by the bright flame of a torch. It was just over his face, held by a stooping figure. Mark blinked to clear his vision and found himself looking up into a wrinkled, haggard, old face covered with a thick, white beard and wild, white hair. "Oh," he said, startled.

47

"How do you fare?" the old man asked. "Can you sit up?"
Mark nodded.

"Well?" the old man demanded.

The demand puzzled Mark until he looked again and realized the old man's eyes seemed a peculiar gray color, as if covered with film. They looked away without seeing. He was blind.

"Yes, I can sit up," Mark said and did, his clothes dripping loudly. "Did you save me?"

"'Twas I, yes," the old man said, clutching the torch.

"But how did you . . . y'know, see me?" Mark asked.

"I didn't see you, lad. I *heard* you," the scratchy voice replied. "After so many years wandering the passageways and corridors of this castle, one knows for what to listen. The well waters do not stir unless there's something in there that does not belong." The old man laughed, then continued, "I thought you were a loose bucket! It is a sign of God's grace in your life that I happened to be here."

"I guess," Mark said. He shook his head and worked his jaw in an attempt to get the water out of his ears.

"Guess? Are you so unsure?" the old man challenged.

"No! I mean . . ." Mark didn't know what he meant and let it go. "Thank you for saving me."

The old man laughed again and said, "But it will be you who saves *me!* You have been sent here. This I know for sure."

Mark shook his head. "Save you? How can I save you?" he asked. "I'm here by accident."

"Accident? There is no such thing!" the old man snorted. "Only fools believe in accidents. You are here by providence!"

"You don't know me or why I'm here!" Mark said. "It was a mistake! Sir Owwen may have been captured, and I would've, too, except I jumped in the well." Mark stood up. "Sir Owwen is in trouble. I have to figure out a way to help him."

"You would not be here unless you were chosen to come," the old man insisted. "You must be the one to free the sword!"

"What sword?" Mark asked.

"The Sword of Scales!" the old man said.

"What!"

"Come along with me," the old man said, hooking a bony finger at him.

****

They crept along dark passageways, the old man leading the way with his torch held high. Mark wanted to ask why he needed a torch if he was blind, but he thought better of it. There's no point in offending your only ally.

"The torch is for you," the old man said suddenly, as if Mark had asked his question out loud. "I knew one day you would come and have kept torches at the ready."

Mark was mystified. "How could you know *I* was going to come? It's just a trip in The Imagination Station. I'm not really part of this."

"You're part of it," the old man said softly. "Even if you don't know what part."

The old man's statement didn't make sense to Mark, nor did he care to pursue it. It was the same sort of riddle Sir Owwen kept saying.

"Where are we going?" Mark asked, changing the subject. "Are we going to get the Sword of Scales? Can we find Sir Owwen?"

"Be patient," the old man said.

"How do you know your way around?" Mark asked.

"A castle like this has many passages that only a blind man could find — because they are hidden behind entryways that deceive the eyes."

Mark persisted. "But how did you wind up here in this castle in the first place?"

The old man explained that a long, long time ago, he was a knight who had been entrusted with the Sword of Scales. "But I was captured by Sir Cardoc on the road to find Slothgrowl. He kept me prisoner along with the sword for more years than I could count. Those years of darkness caused me to go blind. With that, I put on an act of insanity so Sir Cardoc and his henchmen might disregard me. As I'd hoped, they eventually did. But tell me, lad, how it is that you are here?"

Mark told the old man that they came to rescue the son of a widow they met in the forest.

The old man suddenly stopped and turned to face Mark. He nodded and said, "Aye, the story is familiar to me. For that same widow lured me from my quest and sent me to this castle for similar mischief."

"But—how?" Mark asked. "You've been locked in here for years. The woman we met was young."

The old man smiled, then continued on his way. "She is really an enchantress employed by Sir Cardoc," he replied.

"Oh, no," Mark groaned. "Then it's all my fault. Sir Owwen, didn't want to help the widow, but I made him do it. If anything happens to him . . . it'll be my fault."

The old man held up his hand. "Sshh. This is the place." He handed the torch to Mark and pressed his hands against the wall. His fingers moved quickly, finding a gap between two of the stones. "Ah," he whispered and pushed down. Mark heard a soft click—like a latch being lifted—and the old man took the torch back. "Now push."

"Push what?" Mark asked.

"The wall!" the old man replied impatiently.

Mark shrugged but obeyed. He pressed his shoulder against the wall and put all his weight behind his push. To his surprise, the wall swung open like a revolving door.

"Be on the lookout," the old man said as they walked through. "Sometimes a guard comes to check the sword. But the hour is late, and we may hope no one will come."

The room was empty, save for a table and chair with a very old and moldy loaf of bread. Mark started to wonder why the old man had brought him into what looked like a prison cell when he heard a soft humming and saw a glowing light off to the side. He turned in the direction from which the hum and the glow came.

"Oh!" he exclaimed. There on the wall hung the Sword of Scales. It was upside down — making the form of a cross — with a brilliant, silver blade that had intricately carved swirls along its edges. At the top, a gold handle bore words that Mark had to strain to read: *Deus Misereatur.*

"Beautiful beyond words," the old man said.

"What does 'dee-oose miser —'?"

"*Deus misereatur* means 'God be merciful,'" the old man said. "It's Latin."

"Let's grab it and get out of here," Mark suggested.

The old man shook his head. "You may try, but you'll do so at your own risk. The Sword of Scales is held to the wall by enchanted chains. Can you not see them? Only the chosen knight may free it. All others will die in their attempt."

Mark looked more closely and saw a gold fastener just beneath the T of the hilt and another farther down the blade. Whether they were really enchanted wasn't his to guess. "So, picking the lock is a no-go, I guess," he said.

The old man nodded and replied, "Indeed."

"So, who's the chosen knight?" Mark asked.

"It's the one who frees the sword," said the old man.

"Oh, I get it," Mark said, not getting it at all. *More riddles,* he thought.

"Do you feel it within yourself to free the sword? Only if you do will you know if you have the calling as the chosen knight."

"I don't feel anything," Mark said, "except that we should get out of here."

The old man tilted his head and said softly, "In this you are surely right. A guard is coming."

Mark heard the footsteps in the corridor and went bug-eyed. "What are we supposed to do?" Mark asked.

"Hide behind the door and hit him with this!" the old man commanded, throwing something at Mark. Then he sat down at the table.

"A loaf of bread?" Mark asked, unsure that stale dough would make a good weapon. He hid behind the door anyway.

The guard lifted the latch and thrust the door open. "What's this?" he exclaimed when he saw the old man at the table. "What are you doing in here?"

"This is my penance," the old man said. Then he shouted to Mark, "Now!"

Mark sprang from behind the door and hit the guard in the back of the head with the loaf.

The guard said, "Oww!" and turned on Mark.

Mark swallowed hard. Bread wasn't made for knocking the bad guys out.

"That hurt," the guard said as he reached for Mark's neck.

With surprising agility, the old man leapt up from the chair and grabbed the guard from behind. The guard struggled, but the old man's strength was greater than Mark or the guard could have imagined. In a moment, the guard collapsed to the floor.

"Help me," the old man said, grabbing the guard under the arms and dragging him away.

Mark was too stunned to take any action. "How did you do that?"

"Help me!" the old man said urgently. "Put him in the secret passageway."

Mark grabbed the guard's feet, and they did just as the old man commanded. Afterward, they returned to the room, where Mark was instructed to push the wall closed.

"But what are we gonna do now?" Mark asked.

"Come!" said the old man. "We shall find your friend."

"But we don't have any weapons or even a plan!" Mark complained as he followed the old man out of the room.

"Now you must have *faith!*" the old man said.

CHAPTER TEN

A Challenge

Mark was surprised they could walk so freely down the halls and stairwells of the castle. "Where is everybody?" he finally asked.

"In the courtyard for the carnival," the old man answered. "But Sir Cardoc isn't. No doubt he'll be in his throne room making sport of your friend."

"Throne room?" Mark asked. "I thought only kings had throne rooms."

The old man waved a hand. "Sir Cardoc imagines himself a king. Such is the pride of the man — a pride that will work to our purposes, Lord willing."

Mark and the old man reached a doorway, where the old man suddenly stopped. "Take my arm," he said.

Mark did and said, "But what are —"

The old man signaled him to be quiet and listen. From inside the room, they could hear voices. Mark peeked around the corner and felt his heart jump. Sir Cardoc sat in a giant chair, with Sir Owwen standing before him. Nearby stood the widow Mark had seen in the forest, wringing her hands anxiously. She wasn't in the simple peasant's gown she had worn in the forest, but in flowing robes that seemed to move with a breeze, though the air was still.

"I have no sympathy for your king or his causes," Sir Cardoc said, his eyes flashing. "And I would not indulge him to receive the Ring of Uther."

The enchantress — if that's what she was — stepped forward and said, "Enough of this nonsense! This knight had a boy with him whom your incompetent guards have yet to catch!"

"What do I care for a boy?" Sir Cardoc asked.

"You will care when he surprises us with unexpected trouble!" she shouted in return.

Mark was pleased to be the source of her concern. He expected it was the only revenge he would ever have for her deceitfulness.

"Where is the boy?" Sir Cardoc asked. He leaned forward, and his eyes glared viciously. "Did you make some plan to rendezvous?"

"On my word, I do not know where the boy is," Sir Owwen rightly said. "But you must heed me, sir! Even as a fallen knight, you must do honor! I am on a quest for the king. You are duty-bound to free me!"

"Ha! He's *your* king, not mine," Sir Cardoc spat.

"Then, by the traditions of our land, you are duty-bound to allow me a challenge!" Sir Owwen said.

"Fight you? I would not waste my breath or my time!"

Sir Owwen stepped forward. "Confound it! You dishonor yourself, sir! If you will not fight, you must allow me to champion my cause somehow!"

"Perhaps I might make a suggestion!" the old man suddenly shouted. It startled Mark, and he almost didn't hear him add, "Lead me forward, boy."

Mark wanted only to run and hide. "Are you nuts?" he asked.

"Lead me!" he snapped, clutching Mark's arm so tightly that it hurt.

Sir Owwen, Sir Cardoc, and the enchantress were suitably surprised by the appearance of the old man and Mark as they walked toward the throne.

"I warned you!" the enchantress shrieked.

"Quiet, woman!" Sir Cardoc shouted. "He is here with a blind beggar! What harm is it?"

The old man said loudly, "I suggest that the most brave and gallant Sir Cardoc and Sir Owwen might settle their differences in a show of strength."

The enchantress leaned forward. "This is trickery!" she bellowed.

"I said to hold your tongue!" Sir Cardoc growled at her.

The enchantress retreated a few steps. Mark noticed she looked similar to the woman he had seen in the forest, but much older. He wondered how she made herself look so young.

"By what manner do we have this show of strength?" Sir Cardoc asked the old man.

"With swords of choice," the old man cackled. "Both driven into the great stone in the courtyard. Whoever drives his sword farthest wins."

"Wins what? What is the prize?" Sir Cardoc asked suspiciously.

"Freedom, lord. If Sir Owwen wins, we may go free. If Sir Owwen loses, you may do with all of us as you wish."

"Why should I waste my time?" Sir Cardoc snapped.

The old man bowed slightly. "My lord, I do not expect *you* to waste your time. Perhaps you might appoint a strong representative for yourself — to take your place in the contest."

"What!" Sir Cardoc roared. "Let someone else take *my* place in a contest of strength? By my word, old man, I am tempted to strike you down here and now for your insolence!"

"My deepest apologies," the old man said.

"Good sir, you do me great honor speaking on my behalf," Sir Owwen began, darting a glance back and forth between Mark and the old man. "But wouldn't a joust be preferable?"

He's afraid, Mark thought.

The old man said warmly, "Good knight — and in my heart I know you are a *good* knight — take this opportunity."

"Yes!" Sir Cardoc said, jumping to his feet. "I will win this contest, then spend the remainder of the night deciding in what way I will torture, then dispatch, you."

"But I have no sword," Sir Owwen said.

"Incidentals!" Sir Cardoc shouted.

"Our lord Cardoc has agreed that you may choose a sword," the old man said. "Is that right, my lord?"

Sir Cardoc waved his hand impatiently. "Yes, yes," he said.

The old man smiled and said to Sir Owwen, "Then choose . . . the Sword of Scales."

"The Sword of Scales!" Sir Owwen gasped and made the sign of the cross.

The enchantress moved forward, clearly eager to speak but keeping her hand on her mouth.

"It's in a room downstairs," Mark stated. "I saw it."

Sir Owwen turned to Sir Cardoc angrily. "You! You have been hiding the Sword of Scales all these years?"

Sir Cardoc nodded. "Of course," he answered. "And if it is your choice, then I am relieved of my obligation to kill you. Touch that sword, and forces greater than mine will take your life."

"Unless he is the chosen knight," the old man added.

"Are you?" Sir Cardoc asked Sir Owwen.

Mark looked at Sir Owwen's face and wondered if he thought he was.

Sir Owwen lowered his head sadly.

The old man touched his arm gently. "Have faith, my knight," he said.

Sir Owwen lifted his head and gazed intently into the old man's eyes. In a firm voice he said, "I choose the Sword of Scales."

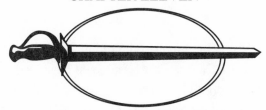

CHAPTER ELEVEN

The Sword of Scales

The room containing the Sword of Scales was exactly as Mark and the old man had left it. Mark listened for any sound from the guard in the hidden passageway. All was silent.

The enchantress eyed Mark cautiously. Mark returned her stare until she looked away. It was a small victory.

They stood beneath the Sword of Scales, its hum and glow warm and comforting.

"I am amused that this will settle our conflict without a contest," Sir Cardoc said. "Perhaps disappointed."

"You are a fool," the enchantress said. "They are using your pride to trick you, to force you into disaster!"

Sir Cardoc angrily swung around, striking the enchantress with the back of his hand. She stumbled, then braced herself against the table. She touched the red mark on her chin lightly and glared at Sir Cardoc. Mark expected her to raise her hand and zap Sir Cardoc with a spell or bolt of lightning or something. Instead, she marched out of the room.

"I have no toleration for intrusive women," Sir Cardoc snarled. He turned to Sir Owwen. "If you're going to take the sword, take it!"

Sir Owwen knelt where he was, murmured softly, then made the sign of the cross once more. He stood up and turned to Mark and the old man. Mark wanted to shout for him not to do it, to run — all of them — as quickly as they could. If Sir Owwen touched the sword and died, Mark would take the blame for the rest of his life. He hadn't forgotten that it was his fault they were in the castle at all.

Sir Owwen reached for the sword, then hesitated. "Only in the Lord am I worthy of anything," he said.

Sir Cardoc began to laugh.

Sir Owwen grabbed the blade of the sword with his right hand. He clutched it so hard, blood appeared around the edges and through his fingers. But he didn't flinch or look as if he felt any pain. He merely tugged at the sword. Mark was aware that the hum had grown louder, and, unless he imagined it, the sword grew brighter and brighter. The fasteners unsnapped, and the sword tipped forward, as if offering Sir Owwen its hilt. Sir Owwen accepted the hilt with his left hand and held it up.

The sword was free.

"No!" Sir Cardoc screamed as he pulled his own sword from his belt and thrust at Sir Owwen.

Sir Owwen was prepared and repelled the thrust with a quick swipe of the Sword of Scales.

Mark pulled the old man back and watched as the two men lunged at each other. Mark was not so much afraid as he was awed by the ferocity of the fight. At one point, both men fell upon the table, getting tangled as it shattered into pieces. They instantly leapt to their feet again and thrashed at each other over and over. They were evenly matched in their skill, though Sir Cardoc employed one or two dirty tricks to throw Sir Owwen off balance.

The duel went on and on, unaffected by the appearance of guards who looked fearful and kept their distance.

"They fear lest they attack the chosen knight who rescued the Sword of Scales and be smitten by God," the old man whispered after Mark told him of the guards' arrival.

It seemed as if Sir Cardoc had the better of Sir Owwen as he strode forward, hacking away at the Sword of Scales held defensively before him. But Sir Owwen suddenly swung along with one of Sir Cardoc's strokes, spun quickly, and brought the Sword of Scales hard against Sir Cardoc's side. The blow sent Sir Cardoc headlong to the ground, and Sir Owwen was instantly upon him, the pointed end of the sword pressed against Sir Cardoc's neck.

"I yield!" Sir Cardoc cried. "Of your mercy, sir, I yield!"

"You yield now, but what of it when my back is turned?" Sir Owwen challenged.

"I swear to you, good knight," Sir Cardoc gasped, "that a stronger and braver man I have never known. Spare me my life and I will be your man, as well as all my noble warriors and servants!"

Sir Owwen laughed long and hard.

Mark was startled. He couldn't remember Sir Owwen ever laughing so jovially.

"I give you your life," Sir Owwen said, but he held the sword firm.

"God bless you, sir," Sir Cardoc said.

"But I have no use for you, your warriors, or your servants," Sir Owwen said. He turned to one of the guards and commanded, "Sir, if you wish to see your master alive, go on horseback and seek out Sir Miles of Brandon. It is he who will lay siege to this castle!"

"No!" Sir Cardoc cried out.

"Yes!" Sir Owwen said. "You yield to me, and I yield to him. He shall hold this castle until the king himself may minister justice and repay you for your cruelty and treachery!"

CHAPTER TWELVE

Into the Woods

I t was dawn by the time Sir Miles secured Sir Cardoc's castle, put Sir Cardoc in his own dungeon, and searched in vain for the enchantress. Sir Miles speculated that she used her powers to hide away. Mark, still skeptical about magic, figured she simply left the castle after Sir Cardoc struck her.

The dew still covered the forest when Mark, Sir Owwen, and the old man left the castle. They walked silently for a mile, then stopped at a fork in the path. The old man then announced that he must go his own way.

Sir Owwen bowed to the old man and took him by the hand. "God bless you, sage," he said. "I owe you my life for your gallant intervention."

The old man placed his hand gently on Sir Owwen. "I did nothing," he replied. "It is your brave heart that saved you. Farewell."

"How can you leave us?" Mark asked. "You were trapped

in the castle so long. I mean, isn't it dangerous for a blind man to wander the woods?"

The old man tilted his head back and laughed a hearty, youthful laugh. As he did, his stooped form seemed to straighten so that he was as tall as Sir Owwen. A dazzling light spun around his garment, turning it into a new robe of white. The age and wrinkles seemed to fall from his face like scales. The filmy, gray eyes became a clear blue.

Mark and Sir Owwen stood like statues, unable to move or react — so brilliant was the display. "What is this sorcery?" Sir Owwen finally asked to no one in particular.

The transformation complete, the man (it would be wrong to call him old now) gestured grandly. "It is not sorcery, but the best kind of wizardry."

"But who — what — are you?" Mark asked.

"Do you not know?" he said with a low chuckle. "Sir Owwen knows."

Mark turned to Sir Owwen, who still stood in wide-eyed amazement. "Who is he?" Mark asked.

"He is Peregrine," Sir Owwen said without blinking. "The king's own prophet and worker of wonders."

"Worker of wonders indeed," Peregrine answered with a smile. "For this is a land of wonder and imagination. I was sent by the king to help you. Now I must take my leave."

"But you were waiting for us in the castle!" Mark said. "How could the king send you to help us? We didn't even know we were going to the castle until the widow tricked us."

"Though you were tricked and chose foolishly, God used your choices for the good of His greater plan!" Peregrine replied.

"But—*how?*" Mark asked.

Peregrine held a hand to his chest and said, "You're asking me to explain to you the mysteries of God? I am a tinkerer, not a priest. It is for Him to know the plan and for us to work it out."

Mark shook his head. He couldn't comprehend it.

"Then, kind Peregrine," Sir Owwen said, "might you know the direction we may take so that the Sword of Scales will find its rightful place in the heart of Slothgrowl and we may release the coveted Ring of Uther?"

Peregrine nodded. "Because of your courage and valor, I have one other message to aid you in your quest. To find Slothgrowl, you must go to the Hall of the Forgotten, where the Gold Book is found. You must break the seal and open the book, then do what it tells you."

"The Hall of the Forgotten?" Mark wondered.

"Farewell, and God speed you in your travels, for you shall not see me again," Peregrine said as he turned away from them. "And remember the signs the king gave you!"

Mark watched him move into the sunlit path—a stooped and ragged old man once again.

****

Sir Owwen knew the way to the Hall of the Forgotten. "It

was once a beautiful chapel," he told Mark. "But our legends tell of a day when a handsome young wizard arrived there to be wed to the most beautiful maiden in the land. On the way to the chapel, the maiden was overcome by brutal marauders who slew her and her entire party of bridesmaids. The wizard was so distraught that he placed a curse on the chapel and the road on which the maiden traveled."

"You have a lot of legends, don't you?" Mark asked wryly.

"In a land like this, anything can happen — and often does. Do you not have wonders in Odyssey?"

Mark smiled. "A few. But nothing like this."

They walked another mile until Sir Owwen stopped and gestured. "Here," he said simply.

Mark looked around but saw no chapel or anything that resembled a building; just forest and an overgrowth of thorny bushes.

"Where?"

Sir Owwen pointed at the thorny bushes. "This way."

"You're kidding," Mark said, touching the tip of a bush that pricked his finger.

"These thorn bushes cover the road to the Hall of the Forgotten," Sir Owwen explained. "They are part of the curse."

"And Peregrine expects us to get through there alive?" Mark asked doubtfully.

"Indeed he does. And indeed we will," Sir Owwen said, pulling the Sword of Scales from its sheath. He began to hack away at the thorn bushes. "Stay behind me."

Mark followed Sir Owwen down the path as he laboriously thrashed at the overgrowth. The bushes seemed alive to Mark. No sooner did Sir Owwen cut them back than they reached out again, like tentative fingers, to touch and prick Mark.

"Ouch!" he cried out again and again.

Sir Owwen's breathing grew harder as he progressed down the path. His cuts and jabs became less convincing. He was getting tired.

"Do you want me to do it for a while?" Mark asked.

Sir Owwen shook his head and replied, "Touch this sword and you will die. And I fear that my knife will be useless against these thorns."

"Then can we stop for a couple of minutes so you can rest?"

Sir Owwen nodded, and they sat down in the clearing they had made. The silence was deafening to Mark, and he soon identified the problem. He didn't hear the normal sounds he would've expected from the woods: tree branches rustling or birds singing.

"The curse," Sir Owwen remarked when Mark asked him about it.

They both closed their eyes, allowing what little sun there was to fall on their faces. But as soon as they did, they felt the sting of the thorn bushes again reaching out, threatening to cover them over. Mark sat up and noticed that the path behind them was completely overrun again.

"Sir Owwen!" Mark cried.

Sir Owwen opened his eyes just as the branch of a bush

reached out to scratch his face. He quickly chopped it with the Sword of Scales. "We must continue," he said. Then he sighed and stood up.

Sir Owwen continued to slash at the bushes, slower but steadily. Mark helped as he could by using Sir Owwen's knife to chop at the outstretched branches.

For Mark, it seemed like hours before they caught sight of the Hall of the Forgotten. It looked like an old church, as Sir Owwen had said, but was crumbled and decayed. The ruins stood like chipped and jagged black teeth in a hideous mouth. Sir Owwen and Mark cleared the bushes and stood on a broken stone path leading to the massive, wooden door that served as entrance.

"The Hall of the Forgotten," Sir Owwen whispered. "A place of great desolation."

"Pretty spooky, too," Mark said.

The stones cracked beneath their feet as they approached the door. Sir Owwen pushed it open and stepped in. Mark held back, momentarily expecting something to jump out at them. When nothing did, he followed closely.

The inside was dark and musty. Cobwebs stretched from pillars to fallen beams, glittering in a shaft of sunlight that shone through a hole in the roof. A small bird flew in, ducked, and flew out again.

The Sword of Scales at the ready, Sir Owwen looked to the left and to the right as they walked the center aisle, between the shattered pews, to the altar. There, on a large, wooden stand, sat a golden book that seemed to sparkle in a light of its own.

"I guess that's the Gold Book," Mark whispered.

"Aye," Sir Owwen whispered back. "It was the book of vows from which the priest would have read the wedding ceremony."

"If it's just a wedding book, how can it tell us what to do next?" Mark asked.

Sir Owwen turned to face Mark. "Have you been here so long and yet you still cannot grasp the mystery of this place? There are times to ask questions and times to accept answers without questions. I do not ask now. I am grateful if this Gold Book can serve us on the king's quest."

As they reached the altar, the sun suddenly disappeared behind a cloud. Mark quickly glanced around, afraid it might be some sort of trap.

"Look!" Sir Owwen said as he pointed at the altar.

The Gold Book's cover turned bright yellow, the seal blazing.

Sir Owwen raised the sword high and brought it down with a hard stroke on the seal. It snapped and fell away. Next, as if moved by an invisible hand, the cover flipped open and fell to the side. Then the pages turned.

A harsh whisper — rather, the sound of hundreds of whispers — filled the room. "Have you brought the Sword of Scales?" they asked.

"I have," Sir Owwen shouted as if to be heard above the eerie sound.

"Touch its tip to the bottom of the Book of Gold!" the whispered voices commanded. They seemed to come from every-where. They sounded as if they were even inside Mark's head. He scanned the room, sure he would see loudspeakers in the corners. He didn't.

Sir Owwen took the Sword of Scales in both hands and placed the tip on the bottom of the book. The book and sword's tip turned red hot as smoke poured upward from the page. It was if someone had taken a hot iron and branded the altar. It hissed loudly.

Mark retreated a step, wanting nothing more than to run. Like the voices, the hiss seemed to fill every space of air. He thought his eardrums might burst.

Then, as suddenly as it started, it stopped, leaving an echo as its only remembrance. Sir Owwen and Mark stood still for a moment. *Is there something else?* Mark wondered.

Sir Owwen obviously decided there wasn't and moved for-ward to the altar. Mark followed. They peered at the page together, its gold edgings now scorched black. Words had been burned into the pages that said:

> The large door will lead you to the place you seek.
> Looking neither to the left nor the right, keep your
> eyes straight ahead or all will be lost.

Mark and Sir Owwen exchanged a curious glance, then turned around to face the sanctuary. They hadn't noticed a large door except the one through which they had entered. Surely it wasn't the one. It led back outside to the thorny path.

Or did it? They both thought the same thing, for they moved together back down the aisle without saying a word.

Sir Owwen reached down to the door handle and grabbed it as if he thought it might leap from his grasp. With a jolt, he yanked the door open.

The thorny path, the forest, the day — all semblance of the outside was gone. Instead, they stared into great darkness.

"Look neither to the left nor the right, but keep your eyes straight ahead — no matter what happens," Sir Owwen reminded Mark.

Mark nodded that he understood.

Sir Owwen took Mark's hand, and they stepped through the door.

CHAPTER THIRTEEN

A Dark Journey

The passageway was pitch black. Mark could only guess how Sir Owwen knew where to walk until he noticed the speck of light that seemed to move just a foot ahead of them. Mark wondered if there were walls to each side and thought about reaching out, but he was afraid of what he might touch — or what might grab him. He didn't dare look. His instructions were clear: look neither to the left nor the right, but keep your eyes straight ahead. He obeyed. It was easy, because the passageway was quiet.

Then the silence turned into a house of horrors. From the left came a terrifying shriek that made Mark's skin crawl. Then, from the right, a soul-shaking yell.

"Keep your eyes straight, lad!" Sir Owwen shouted, lifting the Sword of Scales as if it could protect them.

"I'm trying! I'm trying!" Mark called back.

The screams and yells increased from both sides, as if maniacal ghosts were enticing them to look their way. At first, they only made noises. Then a low voice hollered something at Sir Owwen about a fallen knight named Sir Baudwin whom Sir Owwen had slain unjustly. Sir Owwen trembled and cried out that it wasn't true. Voices from all sides began to shout accusations and abuses at Sir Owwen, most of which Mark didn't understand. But Sir Owwen understood and groaned.

Now they're getting personal, Mark thought.

"Mark! Look over here!" a voice screeched from the right. "It's the door to The Imagination Station! You can get out now!"

Another voice chimed in, "You can finish this adventure and go back to Whit's End! Your parents are waiting for you!"

Mark nearly turned his head, if only to tell the voices to shut up. He resisted the temptation and said over and over to himself, *Keep your eyes straight ahead or you'll be lost.*

"We're moving away!" the voice of his mother said. "You'll never see Odyssey again!"

"Be quiet!" Mark yelled.

His father's voice came to him, low and gentle: "Maybe you'll want to stay in The Imagination Station. Maybe you shouldn't ever return."

"No! You're not my father! Be quiet!" Mark screamed.

"I bid you in the name of our Lord to withdraw!" Sir Owwen growled. "Withdraw!"

The voices faded. Sir Owwen stopped where he was and took a deep breath. Mark rested his head against Sir Owwen's back, his chain mail cold against Mark's forehead. Sir Owwen reached around and patted him with a large hand. "By the grace of God," he said.

"Amen," Mark said.

"There — ahead of us — I spy a gray light," Sir Owwen said. "Come!"

They kept their eyes straight just in case they weren't clear yet. But no other voices rose to taunt or tempt them. The low ceiling forced them to crawl by the time they reached the gray light and what appeared to be the mouth of a cave. Only then did they realize *they* had been in a cave and were now crouched at an opening overlooking a larger one. As Mark glanced at the walls of the large cave, he saw other openings — like railway tunnels drilled into the rock.

"Ah!" Sir Owwen gasped and pointed down at the bottom of the large cave. Mark looked and felt his heart skip a beat. The cave was filled with a vast store of treasure; rubies, diamonds, coins, gold, copper, silver, gems, bracelets, and necklaces all sparkled in the dusty light.

"Wow!" Mark exclaimed and jumped from their perch to a ledge below. He carefully balanced himself on the assorted rocks that led to the cave floor.

"No, lad!" Sir Owwen called in a harsh whisper.

"I just wanna look!" Mark whispered back. And in no time, he found himself thrusting his hands into a chest of gold coins. As he played with the coins, he asked, "How in the world are we going to find that ring you want?"

Sir Owwen followed Mark's path. "We must be careful!" he warned. "Don't you smell it?"

Mark hadn't, and now he took a deep breath. It nearly made him gag. The air was filled with something putrid and smoky. "What—"

Mark's question was cut off by an earsplitting roar. Smoke poured out of a black hole at the rear of the cave.

"Hide!" Sir Owwen said, grabbing Mark's arm. "We're in the den of Slothgrowl!"

CHAPTER FOURTEEN

Slothgrowl

Sir Owwen pulled Mark by the arm, and they knelt behind a large mound of jewels. The cave grew hotter and hotter until it felt as if Mark and Sir Owwen were sitting next to a fiery furnace.

Slothgrowl emerged from the hole and slithered into the cave. His eyes flamed red, and plumes of smoke drifted from the flared nostrils of his long snout. His forked tongue writhed and his teeth gnashed as a blinding flash of fire flew from his mouth. His long body and slick, lizardlike skin squirmed atop short legs and feet with sharp talons. Under his chin, a patch of scales reached down like a shield to his front legs. He moved his head to and fro, as if searching the cave, then crouched in the center and sat very still.

"I know you are here," Slothgrowl said in a low, gurgling voice that turned Mark's stomach. "Your every movement is known to me."

Sir Owwen signaled Mark to stay quiet.

Slothgrowl breathed heavily, snorting flames. "You are to be rewarded for venturing this far. Few have accomplished as much."

Mark wanted to cough from the stench and smoke, but he covered his mouth.

"Perhaps I will give you part of this treasure," Slothgrowl said. "Answer me three questions — only three — and you shall have your freedom and as much of this treasure as you can carry. Do you agree?"

Mark and Sir Owwen stayed silent where they were.

Suddenly Slothgrowl swiped at the mound of jewels, causing large gems to fall on top of them. "Do you believe you are hidden from me? With one breath I could burn you to cinders! Come out and face me!"

Mark looked to Sir Owwen, who stood and walked out, his hand held resolutely on the hilt of the Sword of Scales. Mark trailed after him. Facing Slothgrowl was more horrifying than Mark could have imagined, and he felt his knees go weak at the sight of the monster.

"Much better," Slothgrowl said. "Now answer me three questions and you will have freedom and wealth."

"We have not come all this way for freedom or wealth, but to return the Ring of Uther to its rightful owner," Sir Owwen said boldly.

Slothgrowl laughed — short snorts full of flame and smoke.

"The Ring of Uther, is it? You are wiser to answer my questions and run for your lives than to attempt to capture that ring."

"Say what you will—" Sir Owwen began, but Mark interrupted him.

"What are the questions?" Mark asked. Sir Owwen turned to Mark with surprise. Mark said softly, "Let's stall for time. Maybe we'll figure out where the ring is."

"The boy wants the questions. Do you concur, knight?"

Sir Owwen nodded.

"The first question," Slothgrowl announced, "is simple. By what authority do you come to me?"

Sir Owwen stood tall. "By the authority of the king to reclaim that which is his!" he proclaimed.

Slothgrowl gurgled in what Mark thought was a chuckle. "Very good. For you are a knight of the king and have the right to invoke his name." His forked tongue darted out and back again. "Boy, my next question is for you."

Mark swallowed hard and forced out, "Me?"

Slothgrowl slurped and growled for a moment. "From the deepest part of your heart, tell me: what is the name of your home?"

The question threw Mark for a moment. It was a trick of some sort, he knew. Sir Owwen watched him carefully, his fingers curling around the hilt of the Sword of Scales. "Do you mean Odyssey or Washington?" Mark asked.

Slothgrowl spat a short flame and roared, "You do not ask me questions! Tell me, from your heart, the name of your home!"

"From my heart . . ." Mark began, wondering how Sloth-growl knew to ask him a personal question and knowing for sure that it was a trick. His home could be in Odyssey or in Washington. How could Mark answer? And then he realized *it didn't matter* whether his home was in Odyssey or Washington.

"You do not have an answer!" Slothgrowl said happily.

"I have an answer," Mark said. "My home is wherever my parents are."

Slothgrowl scowled and stomped his feet up and down angrily in what Mark perceived to be a tantrum. Smoke poured from his nostrils, and fire escaped from both sides of his mouth. But Slothgrowl couldn't deny the answer. He knew Mark was speaking truthfully from his heart.

Sir Owwen placed a hand on Mark's shoulder. "Well done, lad," he said. "Confounding a dragon is no easy thing."

Then Slothgrowl roared out the third question: "How will you kill me? For if you do not kill me, you will die!"

Sir Owwen answered by drawing the Sword of Scales.

Slothgrowl reared back with an expression of surprise, then stood firm with renewed confidence. "That sword is no good to you unless you know how to use it," he snarled. "Do you know?"

"That's four questions," Mark said glibly.

Slothgrowl blasted them with a burst of flames. Mark and Sir Owwen dove behind a large chest of gold nuggets just in time. When it seemed safe, they sprang to their feet and wove their way deeper into the mountains of treasure.

"You cannot hide from me!" Slothgrowl roared. From the sounds of his shuffling and the crashes that followed, he was obviously searching for them.

"You can kill him with the Sword of Scales, right?" Mark whispered.

Sir Owwen looked worried. "The fiend is right. I do not possess the knowledge to use the sword properly."

"Can't you just stab him with it?"

"I could try," Sir Owwen said, and before Mark could stop him, he scurried over a mound of statues. Mark stood up and peered over in time to see Sir Owwen leap upon Slothgrowl's back. Slothgrowl instantly began to twist and turn to toss the knight off. Before he could, Sir Owwen raised the sword high and brought it down once — twice — three times into Slothgrowl's back. A green slime spilled out like blood. Slothgrowl threw his head back and lurched so severely that Sir Owwen flew into another stack of treasure.

Mark watched as Slothgrowl stopped and closed his eyes. *He's hurt!* Mark thought.

But the hope was premature. While Mark looked on wide-eyed, the wounds on Slothgrowl's back closed, the green slime stopped flowing, and within a minute it looked as if he'd never been stabbed.

"You dishonor your king," Slothgrowl said. "As the chosen knight, you should know how to use the Sword of Scales. Now you will know only death."

Slothgrowl moved toward a stunned Sir Owwen. He was sure to burn him to a crisp.

"No!" Mark jumped to the top of the statues and began to throw the smaller busts, like rocks, at Slothgrowl's head. Slothgrowl turned to Mark. It gave Sir Owwen enough time to throw himself behind another heap of treasure, but Mark wasn't so fortunate. With lightning speed, Slothgrowl flicked his tail at Mark, knocking him head over heels through the air. He landed with a thump onto the hard floor of the cave. The fall knocked the wind out of him.

"This is a tiresome game," Slothgrowl said.

Mark struggled to sit up and leaned against a tall box, clutching his side, gasping for air. Sir Owwen crept toward him, the sword poised in case Slothgrowl appeared.

"I have failed," Sir Owwen whispered. "God grant me a quick death. The Sword of Scales is useless against the beast."

"But I don't get it," Mark groaned. "There must be a way. What's the point of having a special sword unless it —"

Slothgrowl slithered around the edge of the treasure and stood before them. His eyes burned furiously, and a line of greenish drool slipped from his mouth and slid across the scales on his chest. "I will delight in picking your bones," he said.

Mark closed his eyes, but the image of the scales on Slothgrowl's chest hung like a picture inside his eyelids. The scales. They looked like an invincible chest plate, but . . .

Mark opened his eyes as Sir Owwen stood up, ready to fight the monster to his dying breath.

"The scales!" Mark said. "The sword's name!"

Sir Owwen glanced at Mark, then the sword. His expression reflected his understanding, and he shouted loud and mightily—enough to stop Slothgrowl, who looked at Sir Owwen curiously.

"The last herald of defeat?" Slothgrowl asked.

Sir Owwen threw himself at Slothgrowl, the Sword of Scales held forward. Slothgrowl took in a deep breath. *This is it*, Mark thought. *He'll breathe in, then breathe out enough fire to blast us.*

But Slothgrowl's chest, puffed out as it was, made a perfect target. Sir Owwen thrust the sword into the scales, driving so hard that it sunk to the hilt. Unlike the wounds to his back, Slothgrowl felt this, spewing a great flame into the sky and crying so terribly that the ground shook.

Sir Owwen withdrew the sword, then thrust it in again. Slothgrowl reared back onto his hind legs while his front legs tried desperately to claw at the sword. They were too short to reach the fatal instrument. Slothgrowl twisted onto his side and fell over, gasping and wheezing. His head turned upward, and he spat a small flame, then exhaled as his eyes rolled up into their sockets. He was dead.

Sir Owwen collapsed where he was and, on his knees, thanked God loudly for the victory. Mark whispered his own thanks and stood up.

"Now all we have to do is look for the Ring of Uther,"

Mark said, wondering how they would find it with the glittering treasure all around them.

"It is possible," Sir Owwen suggested, "that the Sword of Scales will assist us." He climbed to his feet, walked over to the slain dragon, and pulled the sword out. An awful smell escaped from the gaping wound and filled the air. Then the dragon began to tremble and shake. The cave echoed with a loud hiss and crackle, as if someone had dropped an egg in a hot frying pan. Still trembling and shaking, the dragon's body turned bright red as if burning from internal heat. Then the bloated skin puckered and shriveled, collapsing inward as it turned black. *Pop!* And in a puff of black and green smoke, the dragon was reduced to ashes.

Mark and Sir Owwen approached the ashes warily and looked down. It was as if someone had dropped the contents of a fireplace onto the ground — such was the lasting glory of Slothgrowl's life.

The light caught a glint in the dark remains. Mark thought it was his imagination and nearly turned away. But it sparkled again, and he knelt down to see what it was. "Sir Owwen?"

Sir Owwen also knelt and, afraid to touch the smoldering ashes, poked at them with the Sword of Scales. He found the source of the sparkle and pushed the tip of the sword through the small loop. It was a ring.

In fact, it was *the* ring — the Ring of Uther.

"God be praised!" Sir Owwen said with a laugh as he held the sword up. "Slothgrowl kept it with him!"

Mark took the ring from the sword tip and looked at it. It was unimpressive to Mark's eyes: a simple, gold ring with an emerald mounted on top. He handed it to Sir Owwen, who took it reverently and held it close. A tear formed in the corner of his eye.

"My quest is completed," Sir Owwen said quietly.

It took a while for them to find their way out of Sloth-growl's den. There were so many holes and tunnels, it was difficult to tell which one led outside. Eventually, a fresh breeze in one of the tunnels gave them a clue, and they crawled out, emerging in the middle of the forest next to a moss-covered knoll. Through the trees, Mark could see the Hall of the Forgotten.

Suddenly, the ground began to shake violently beneath them. "What's this?" Sir Owwen muttered.

"Do you get earthquakes in this country?" Mark asked.

They clung first to each other, then stumbled over to a large tree and grabbed hold. Bits of debris fell from the trees, and a loud crashing sound drew their attention to the Hall of the Forgotten. The ground seemed to swallow it whole.

The knoll from which they had emerged also collapsed, leaving no trace that it ever existed as an entrance to Sloth-growl's den.

The rumbling stopped, and shortly afterward, birds began to sing in the trees.

"Perhaps the curse is lifted," Sir Owwen said.

CHAPTER FIFTEEN

To the King

I t took a full day, a night, and part of another day for Mark and Sir Owwen to reach the king's castle. From a distance, it shone like a beacon from atop a large hill. And that was only a hint of its magnificence as Mark and Sir Owwen approached. The walls were made of a strange, white stone, and the towers and turrets sparkled as if made from diamonds. Men and women dressed in colorful raiment went about their business, calling a cheerful greeting to Sir Owwen by name.

"The castle and surrounding village are called Carleone," Sir Owwen explained. "It is by far the most pleasant of places to be."

At the castle gate, Sir Owwen stopped and told Mark to hold out his hand. Mark did. Sir Owwen placed the Ring of Uther in his palm. "For you to present to the king," he said.

"No," Mark protested. "It was *your* quest! You should give it to him! Besides, I might drop it or something stupid like that."

"It is for you to present," Sir Owwen insisted.

"Why?" Mark asked.

Sir Owwen said, "The final sign."

Mark looked at him quizzically. "There's a final sign? What is it?"

"From boy to king, from the brave to the strong," Sir Owwen recited.

Mark shook his head. "I'm a boy, but I'm not brave," he said. "All I've done is complain and gripe. In fact, I still don't understand why we went through all that trouble for a ring the king could've picked up at any jeweler's."

Sir Owwen smiled wearily at Mark. "There are things in this life that are beyond our understanding, things over which we have no control. Ours is to do what is right and honorable — to obey our master."

"I'm not worthy," Mark said, blushing as he looked at the gate again.

"Come," Sir Owwen said, "we must announce ourselves to the king."

****

Mark thought they would go straight in to the king, and he hastily sweated through the details of how he should act. *What should I say when I give him the ring?* he wondered. *Do I bow? Do I kneel? Do I shake his hand?*

But Mark and Sir Owwen were ushered into the king's private chambers and asked to wait while the king took care of some "affairs of state." As the minutes ticked into an hour, then another, Mark didn't care whether he should bow or kneel. He just wanted to hand over the ring and get something to eat.

Sir Owwen stood by a window that overlooked a vast, green field. Mark suspected he wanted to be rid of his armor and chain mail so he could stroll in the sunshine.

"Are you glad to be home?" Mark asked.

Sir Owwen continued to stare out of the window. "This is not my home," he said.

"Then where —"

"Home is where my king sends me," Sir Owwen replied, a hint of a smile forming at the edges of his lips.

"What if the king sends you somewhere you don't want to be?" Mark asked.

Sir Owwen turned to Mark. "The king could never send me where I do not want to go," he said. "If it is his desire for me to go, then it is my desire as well."

The door leading to the hallway creaked open. Mark and Sir Owwen watched it expectantly. Mark leapt to his feet and almost dropped the ring.

It wasn't the king. It was Peregrine.

"Hello, my friends," Peregrine said, his white hair and robes rustling as if moved by a breeze, though the air was still.

"Peregrine!" Mark said happily.

Sir Owwen bowed slightly.

Peregrine crossed the room to them and smiled as he said,

"Congratulations for your victory over Slothgrowl! The entire land is talking of it!"

"All glory to God," Sir Owwen said.

Peregrine held up his hand and coughed gently. "The king is most anxious about the ring. You *do* have it?"

"Right here," Mark said, holding up his hand.

"Ah," Peregrine said, eyeing the jewel in Mark's palm. "The king asked me to receive it from you for safekeeping."

"As his highness wishes," Sir Owwen said and nodded to Mark.

Peregrine reached forward to take the ring.

Suddenly, Mark closed the ring into his fist and withdrew it. "No," he said.

Peregrine frowned. "What is this?" he asked.

"I can't give it to you," Mark said.

"Be mindful, lad," Sir Owwen said, looking at Peregrine uneasily.

"But I *can't*," Mark maintained.

"Boy, it is not wise to challenge the king's wizard," Peregrine said.

Sir Owwen stepped toward Mark. "Listen to him, lad," he urged.

Mark took a step back. "I can't," he insisted. "You know I can't. The final sign said 'From a boy to a king.' That means I'm supposed to give it to him personally, right? Peregrine isn't the king."

"Oh, stop quibbling," Peregrine snapped irritably. "The king said to get the ring from you, so give it to me!"

"I beseech you, lad," Sir Owwen said, "give the wizard the ring. It is as good as if the king were receiving it."

"No," Mark said defiantly. "It isn't. That isn't what the sign said. It doesn't make sense."

Peregrine waved a hand at Sir Owwen. "He's your charge, Sir Owwen. Deal with him!"

Sir Owwen looked helplessly at Peregrine, then warned Mark, "I will forcibly relieve you of the ring if I must."

"But it doesn't make sense!" Mark cried, backing away from them. "It's some kind of trick. Maybe the king is testing us. It doesn't fit the sign, and—"

"Mark, please!" Sir Owwen implored.

Then Mark remembered one other detail and pressed himself—and his fist—against the wall. "In the forest, when we said good-bye to Peregrine," he began.

"What of it?" Peregrine growled.

"Peregrine said he wouldn't see us again! Don't you remember, Sir Owwen? This is a trick!"

Sir Owwen looked at Peregrine.

"The boy is wrong!" Peregrine shouted.

"If he is wrong, then I am wrong as well. I remember those very words," Sir Owwen said, and instantly he had the Sword of Scales unsheathed and pointed at the stranger before them.

"No!" the stranger yelled. "It is a mistake!"

"Can you maintain your countenance in the brilliance of the Sword of Scales?" Sir Owwen challenged.

"You are wrong!" the stranger cried in a voice much higher than before.

Sir Owwen brought the tip of the sword closer to the stranger's face. "Am I?"

The stranger backed away, the appearance of Peregrine shifting and changing with each step. "Stay away!"

"Reveal yourself!" Sir Owwen commanded.

The stranger spun around and raced for the door, his clothes transforming from the white robes of Peregrine to the red robes of someone else. Someone familiar.

"Stop!" Sir Owwen shouted. But the figure ran on. Sir Owwen lifted the Sword of Scales and threw it just as the stranger reached the door. Mark couldn't be sure if Sir Owwen did it on purpose, but the hilt of the sword, rather than the blade, struck the retreating figure on the back of the head. It slammed the body against the wall, and then both fell to the ground in a heap.

Mark and Sir Owwen ran to the crumpled figure. It was the enchantress from Sir Cardoc's castle.

"In the name of all things that are good and decent!" Sir Owwen said as he picked up the sword. "Your days of treachery are ended." He stood above the enchantress, ready to run her through.

Mark was certain he would have if the door hadn't swung open and the king himself walked through.

"Guards!" the king called in a deep, warmly resonant voice. Three men entered in response and waited. "Shackle this witch until I decide what to do with her!"

As one man, the three guards moved to the enchantress and carried her through the door.

"On your lives, do not let her fool you with her trickery!" the king added before they left.

The king put his hands on his hips and smiled at Mark and Sir Owwen. He was at least a head taller than Sir Owwen, with broad shoulders and a powerful build evident under the gray chain mail and white tunic with the emblem of a red dragon emblazoned on the front. His eyes danced with hidden secrets, and his face was perfectly smooth except for a salt-and-pepper-colored goatee. His hair, flowing onto his shoulders, had a similar coloring. A gold crown adorned his head.

"My liege!" Sir Owwen said as he knelt.

Mark knelt, too, not only because Sir Owwen did, but also because it seemed the only thing anyone could do in front of such a man.

"Arise, Sir Owwen! Arise, young Mark!" the king said.

He knows my name! Mark thought excitedly.

"You have had quite an adventure," the king said. "I commend you for your diligence on my behalf and the wisdom with which you accomplished your quest."

Funny, Mark thought. *He sounds a little like Whit.*

Sir Owwen lowered his head and admitted, "We were not always wise, my lord."

The king clasped his hands behind his back and paced around them thoughtfully. "No, you were not," he said. "But still, all things worked together for the good. You acted according to plan, leading to God's ultimate aim."

Mark, standing now, dared to ask, "But your highness, what *was* the ultimate aim?"

The king laughed and answered, "To show you how God's sovereignty works, of course."

"What!"

Sir Owwen smiled.

The king continued, "It was to teach you about obedience even when you don't know everything. To demonstrate how choices are freely made, yet still fulfill God's plan."

"Wait a minute," Mark said. "You mean all this was done for *me?* But that's impossible! How could I be part of the plan when I don't even belong here? I just dropped in because of The Imagination Station."

The king stood directly in front of Mark, their eyes locking. "Even *that* was part of the plan. This kingdom—*all* king-doms — are under God's subjection."

Mark scratched his head. "But what about the ring?" he asked.

"The ring," the king repeated. "The ring is important to me because it was the ring of my father, Uther. With it, my claim to the throne is complete. May I have it now?"

All of Mark's planning for a formal presentation disappeared as he simply reached out and dropped the ring into the king's hand. The king looked at it pensively.

"It doesn't look so special," Mark said. "I mean, not like my grandfather's watch or something like that."

The king smiled and held the ring up. With his free hand, he grabbed the emerald between his fingers and flipped it to the side on a small, secret hinge. "Do you see the king's seal?" he asked.

Mark looked closer. On the ring itself was the emblem of a red dragon—identical to the one on the king's tunic. It had been hidden beneath the emerald. "Wow," Mark said.

"In days of old, long before I was born, Peregrine wrote my name on the underside of the emerald, lest my kingship be challenged."

Mark squinted to see. Sure enough, the name was there. It said simply, "Arthur."

"You're *King Arthur?*" Mark gasped.

The king nodded and said with a laugh, "I am." He turned to Sir Owwen and called his name.

Sir Owwen bowed.

"As a reward for your obedience and bravery, I entreat you to join us as a knight of the Round Table!" the king said.

Sir Owwen took the king's hand and kissed it. "If it pleases my lord!" he said.

"Indeed it does!" the king answered. "And you, Mark—"

Mark looked up hopefully into the king's face.

"You played your part well," the king said. "You now have

learned a lesson I hope you'll remember in the adventures ahead."

"Adventures ahead?" Mark asked, his mind filling with further quests and encounters with dragons and evil knights and —

The king put his hand on Mark's shoulder. "The adventures that await you — and your parents," he added.

Sir Owwen stood again and said, "You have the heart for it, lad. Whatever awaits you, you have the heart." He put his hand on Mark's other shoulder. Mark felt as if he were being blessed somehow.

Then the room went completely black.

CHAPTER SIXTEEN

The End

"I'm going to have to work on it," Whit said as Mark climbed out of The Imagination Station. "It shouldn't just turn off like that."

Mark stretched his stiff arms and legs. "How long was I in there?" he asked.

"Oh, less than an hour, I think," Whit said as he began to tinker with a control panel on the back of the machine.

Mark looked around the workroom, then at his friend Whit as he fiddled with the knobs and levers. None of it seemed real to him. It was as if his adventure was the real world and this was the make-believe. He said so to Whit.

Whit stopped fiddling and looked at Mark. "This *isn't* the real world, Mark," Whit said. "It's a temporary stage, just like those makeshift stages you see at the theater. We're not meant to stay here—any more than you could have stayed in The

Imagination Station. It's what the apostle Paul means when he talks about setting your sights on things that are eternal. 'For the things we can see are only temporary, but the invisible are eternal.' "

Mark pondered this idea silently for a moment.

Whit leaned against the machine and tucked a screwdriver into his pocket. "That's why I thought you needed this adventure. So you could see how all we do and say fits into a much bigger plan—an eternal plan that comes from God. Whether you live here or in Washington, D.C., your job is to do what's right—to play out your part—to the best of your abilities."

Mark nodded. He got that message loud and clear. But could he do it? Could he say good-bye to his friends in Odyssey and return with his family to Washington?

Home is where my parents are.

The words echoed in his head.

You have the heart for it, Sir Owwen had said.

"I think I can do it," Mark affirmed.

"It won't be easy," Whit said. "But the great adventures rarely are."

"I know."

Mark hugged Whit and walked out of the workroom, up the stairs . . . and out of Whit's End.

About the Author

Paul McCusker is producer, writer, and director for the Adventures in Odyssey audio series. He is also the author of a variety of popular plays including *The First Church of Pete's Garage, Pap's Place*, and co-author of *Sixty-Second Skits* (with Chuck Bolte).

Other Works by the Author

NOVELS:
>*Strange Journey Back* (Focus on the Family)
>*High Flyer with a Flat Tire* (Focus on the Family)
>*The Secret Cave of Robinwood* (Focus on the Family)
>*Behind the Locked Door* (Focus on the Family)
>*Lights Out at Camp What-a-Nut* (Focus on the Family)

INSTRUCTIONAL:
>Youth Ministry Comedy & Drama:
>>*Better Than Bathrobes But Not Quite Broadway*
>>(with Chuck Bolte; Group Books)

PLAYS:
>*Pap's Place* (Lillenas)
>*A Work in Progress* (Lillenas)
>*Snapshots & Portraits* (Lillenas)
>*Camp W* (Contemporary Drama Services)
>*Family Outings* (Lillenas)
>*The Revised Standard Version of Jack Hill* (Baker's Plays)
>*Catacombs* (Lillenas)
>*The Case of the Frozen Saints* (Baker's Plays)
>*The Waiting Room* (Baker's Plays)
>*A Family Christmas* (Contemporary Drama Services)
>*The First Church of Pete's Garage* (Baker's Plays)
>*Home for Christmas* (Baker's Plays)

SKETCH COLLECTIONS:
>*Short Skits for Youth Ministry* (with Chuck Bolte; Group Books)
>*Sixty-Second Skits* (with Chuck Bolte; Group Books)
>*Void Where Prohibited* (Baker's Plays)
>*Some Assembly Required* (Contemporary Drama Services)
>*Quick Skits & Discussion Starters* (with Chuck Bolte; Group Books)
>*Vantage Points* (Lillenas)
>*Batteries Not Included* (Baker's Plays)
>*Souvenirs* (Baker's Plays)
>*Sketches of Harvest* (Baker's Plays)

MUSICALS:
>*The Meaning of Life & Other Vanities*
>>(with Tim Albritton; Baker's Plays)

Other Books by Paul McCusker in the
Adventures in Odyssey® Series

Strange Journey Back

Mark Prescott hates being a newcomer in the small town of Odyssey. And he's not too thrilled about his only new friend being a girl. That is, until Patti tells him about a time machine called the Imagination Station at Whit's End. Mark is sure he can use the machine to bring his separated parents together again, if only he can get past the time machine's eccentric inventor, John Avery Whittaker. This is a story about friendship, responsibility, and living with change.

High Flyer with a Flat Tire

Joe Devlin is accusing Mark Prescott of slashing the tire on his new bike. Mark didn't do it, but how can he prove his innocence? Only by finding the real culprit! With the help of his wise friend, Whit, Mark untangles the mystery and learns new lessons about friendship and family ties.

The Secret Cave of Robinwood

Mark Prescott promises his friend Patti that he will never reveal the secret of her hidden cave. But when the Israelites, a gang Mark wants to join, are looking for a new clubhouse, Mark thinks of the cave. It would be a perfect place. But he promised. Will he betray the hideaway? Will he risk his friendship with Patti? Mark learns about faithfulness, the need to belong, and the gift of forgiveness.

Behind the Locked Door

Mark Prescott's imagination is going wild. Why does his friend John Avery Whittaker keep his attic door locked? What's hidden up there? While staying with Whit, Mark grows curious when Whit forbids him to go behind the locked door. Mark learns hard lessons about trust, honesty, and the need to guard his thoughts.

Lights Out at Camp What-a-Nut

Mark Prescott is not a happy camper. He went to camp so he could talk with his best friend, Patti. But all she wants to do is talk about her new boyfriend. Then Mark finds out he's in the same cabin with Joe Devlin, Odyssey's biggest bully. Joe gets Mark into trouble with the camp's leaders. Finally, Mark and Joe are paired in a treasure hunt that puts them in unexpected danger. Mark learns about how God uses one person to help another.

Breakaway
With colorful graphics, hot topics and humor, this magazine for teen guys helps them keep their faith on course *and* gives the latest info on sports, music, celebrities . . . even girls. Best of all, this publication shows teens how they can put their Christian faith into practice and resist peer pressure.

Clubhouse
Here's a fun way to instill Christian principles in your children! With puzzles, easy-to-read stories and exciting activities, *Clubhouse* provides hours of character-building enjoyment for kids ages 8 to 12.

All magazines are published monthly except where otherwise noted. For more information regarding these and other resources, please call Focus on the Family at (719) 531-5181, or write to us at Focus on the Family, Colorado Springs, CO 80995.